THE
YELLOW COTTAGE
VINTAGE MYSTERIES

THE
CURSE OF
ARUNDEL HALL

BOOK 2

J. NEW

BOOKS BY J. NEW

The Yellow Cottage Vintage Mysteries in order:

The Yellow Cottage Mystery (Free)
An Accidental Murder
The Curse of Arundel Hall
A Clerical Error
The Riviera Affair
A Double Life

The Finch & Fischer Mysteries in order:

Decked in the Hall
Death at the Duck Pond

For Wendy.

THE
CURSE OF
ARUNDEL HALL

CHAPTER ONE

It was never my intention to begin what can now only be described as a career in detective work. I fell into the role of amateur sleuth quite by accident.

My younger brother Jerry and I had grown up in an exceptionally happy and carefree environment. Father owned a textile mill and was the main employer in the area, so as befitted a man of his standing in the community, our house was large. I remember us vividly racing up and down the halls on our bicycles with Patch, our little Jack Russell terrier, snapping at the back wheels.

For afternoon tea on Sundays, unless we'd been invited out, we always toasted our own crumpets on the fire in the small sitting room at the back of the house, then played games as a family until supper, after which we children went to bed.

Christmas had always been a magical time and, in my childish memory, every one of them was white. Large fluffy flakes had drifted lazily down from the sky to cover our lawns and trees in a blanket of snow, and there was always a robin redbreast bobbing up and down on the frozen birdbath, usually stalked by our tom cat Moses. Although being old and rickety of joint, he was never quite fast enough to catch the little bird.

While Christmas Eve and Christmas Day were for the family, for as long as I could remember, Boxing Day was set aside for the workers. After the church service, everybody would trudge back up the snow-filled lane to our house. Invariably, Mother and Father would lead the procession, alongside Jack Scotton, my father's foreman, with his wife and Mr. Pearson the accountant. After that would come the rest of the adult workers, leaving Jerry and me to run back and forth playing with the other children. To me it seemed as though the whole town had been invited.

Once we'd reached the house, the large oak front door would be flung open to welcome our guests and the party would begin. Gifts were given from my family to each of the workers to say thank you for all their hard work that year, and then we'd move to the large dining hall where cook had laid out a sumptuous cold buffet. She'd been preparing it all for days beforehand and for much of that time Jerry and I were camped in the kitchen, where we helped to clean out the bowls and relieve her of any extras. When it was all done, she too took some well-deserved time off and joined in the festivities.

My parents were well-liked and respected by those who worked for them, and this was never more apparent than one day, when I was almost seventeen and Jerry was fifteen, and our lives would forever be changed.

Mother had sheltered us from a lot of what went on, but even then both of us were aware something wasn't quite right. Father was closeted in his study more often and no longer joined us for Sunday tea. There were many times he didn't arise from his bed until after lunch and, as he'd always been an earlier riser, this was particularly unusual. When he did get up, he'd spend his time staring into the fire in the sitting room, morose and silent. What food Mother managed to tempt him with he either barely nibbled at or left completely, and as a result he lost a considerable amount of weight. Eventually, Mother sat us down and explained he'd lost the factory. Even then, with the shock of those words, Jerry and I still didn't fully comprehend the far-reaching implications.

Father, it had turned out, had been caught up in an investment opportunity for which he'd put up the factory as collateral. The investment, while genuine, had failed and as a result he'd lost everything. With the loss of the factory came the loss of our income and as a result we'd had to sell the house and move. But that wasn't the worst of it. Two weeks later, my father, suffering from pneumonia and with his will to live eroded by the guilt of what had happened, passed away.

The funeral was held in the local church and the entire factory workforce came to pay their last respects. For the last time we trudged up the lane to our house and threw open the door to receive our guests. Many wonderful stories were told of Father that day, most of which my brother and I had never heard, and many tears were shed. My father was loved and would be missed by many, but by none more than the three of us.

Later that evening, when everyone else had departed, Jack Scotton and Mr. Pearson remained with Mother, each assuring her they would do all they could to help. Word had obviously spread about our straitened circumstances. True to their word, the very next day both men reappeared to inform her they had negotiated a very favourable deal for us for the sale of the house.

Less than a month later, with the house packed up and everything that hadn't been sold safely in storage, the three of us left our home for the last time. We were to spend the next two and a half years with Aunt Margaret over seventy miles away in Sheffield.

Life with Aunt Margaret more often than not ran smoothly and in the main we all rubbed along quite amicably, but the underlying worry for both of them was of course me and Jerry. Without a paternal figure in his life (Aunt Margaret had never married) and with no business to inherit, Jerry's future was of constant concern to my mother and her sister. However they need not have worried, as Jerry won a scholarship to study "modern greats" at Oxford, and a promising future was assured.

This of course left me, and on that subject the sisters were divided.

My aunt, even with numerous suitors of good pedigree competing for her hand, was a spinster by choice and lived life to its fullest. She had a sharp mind and a rapier wit and was an avid people watcher, as well as a fan of puzzles, having had several of her own published in The Times.

I learned many invaluable lessons at her side and owe much of my success as a detective to her. She was of the opinion I should be left to follow in her footsteps if I wished, and take control of my own life. My mother, on the other hand, was of the opinion a 'suitable match' for me should be found at the earliest opportunity, and no matter how much I pleaded with her on this, she would not budge.

So followed a mind-numbing round of dinner parties and afternoon teas, where I would find myself thrust in front of bored, patronising or over-excitable young men, with whom I had nothing in common and no interest whatsoever. My mother had all but lost hope when I met John, not at one of her interminable soirées, but at a small local bookshop.

We hit it off immediately and after several clandestine meetings, I eventually brought him home to meet the family. Needless to say my mother was ecstatic, my aunt less so, although I paid it little heed at the time. Love is blind as they say, and I was certainly in love. After a courtship and engagement lasting just over a year, John and I were married in the local parish church. I was twenty-one-years-old.

At twenty-three I would become a widow.

After the reported death of my husband, I was advised by his employer to move away from the North of England, take back my maiden name and, aged twenty-three, begin my life again.

"It's for your own safety, Ella," the Home Secretary had said, as we sat in front of a crackling fire, in the parlour of the house John and I had called home for just two short years.

"But I don't understand, Lord Carrick," I choked out over the walnut-sized lump in my throat. "John was just a junior minister for trade. He told me he was helping rebuild our foreign exports to offset the cost of the war. How can that be dangerous to either him or me?"

I'll never forget the withering look on Lord Carrick's face. It was only there fleetingly before he carefully masked his features, but I knew what I'd seen. Pity, tinged with a little guilt perhaps, but it was the scorn and superciliousness that imprinted themselves on my brain. I'd been a naive fool, and at that precise moment, I knew my husband and the life we'd shared together was as artificial as the vase of flowers on the windowsill.

Cast adrift from my home for the second time, I spent the following year with my aunt and my mother while I grieved and contemplated my future.

Often I took the train down to Oxford, booked into a small hotel and spent a few days catching up with my brother. It was during one of these visits that the subject of Linhay came up, which completely changed the course of my life.

It was a glorious summer day, the sky was blue and a warm breeze rustled gently through the foliage. We were enjoying a rather impressive afternoon tea in the gardens of the Trout Inn at Godstow. An impeccably dressed waiter hovered in the background waiting to replenish our cups at a discreet nod. I watched as a punting party came into view under the bridge, and a hand rose, waving at Jerry who returned it with a lazy salute.

"Bickerstaff," he informed me. "His father has a place on Linhay. Invited me down a couple of times, but haven't had a chance to take him up on it yet. Do you remember it?"

"Of course, the yellow cottage," I whispered. I felt my heartbeat increase and a bubble of excitement begin in the pit of my stomach. I knew events thus far had stacked together perfectly to bring me to this pivotal moment. After a year of searching, I realised the island was where I needed to go.

Without knowing it, I was about to embark on a life of murder and mystery.

CHAPTER TWO

The promise of a lovely spring morning had me up and at my desk by seven-thirty. The desk had been my father's, and with her sudden move to the south of France, my mother had had it sent on to me.

"Your father would be pleased to know you had it, darling," she'd said. "He knew how much you loved it."

She was right. The desk was a beautiful oak roll-top with one slim drawer above the knee-hole and three deeper ones down either side. The interior had several cubbyholes, doors and drawers, and the legs were brass capped, culminating in casters that made manoeuvrability simple. Jolly useful when one lived alone.

My original idea when moving to the cottage five months ago was to have a small study area under the stairs. However, with the delivery of the desk, which was far too big for the space, I had moved to the sitting room at the back of the house next to the picture window. There, I could gaze at the garden and the lawns which sloped gently to the river below.

As I was finishing off some last minute correspondence, there was a gentle tap at the door.

"Come in, Mrs. Shaw."

"Apologies for disturbing you, Miss Bridges, but here's this morning's post." She handed me a small bundle held together with a rubber band.

A quick glance at the writing showed me one was from my mother and the other from my aunt, who sent me a new puzzle to solve once a month.

"The postman is waiting to see if you have anything for him to take back?"

"Well, that's very kind of him, but I'm going to the village later, so I will take them myself. Please do pass on my thanks though, Mrs. Shaw."

"Of course, Miss Bridges," she replied, then left, closing the door gently behind her.

Esther Shaw was a tall stocky woman with short iron-grey hair, an almost military bearing in both stance and attitude, and had been in my employ as housekeeper-cum-cook for just over a fortnight. I'd thought it wise to advertise away from the island, small village gossip being what it was, and had placed an advertisement in The Lady Magazine. Surprisingly, hers was the only application I had received. She came directly from employment as housekeeper in a large London home, and said she was used to a busy household where guests dropped in unannounced expecting to be accommodated, and large dinner parties were held on a regular basis. I questioned the fact she might find life in my employ too quiet and rather dull, becoming disillusioned, but she assured me that was what had appealed most about the job. Even though the advert had disappointingly only garnered one applicant, I came to the conclusion Mrs. Shaw was eminently suited to the position. So after a telephone call to her employers, in which they informed me of her excellent credentials and business-like approach to work, along with the fact she was both discreet and honest, I offered her the position and she accepted immediately.

The last two weeks had proved my decision to take her on had been a good one. She was trustworthy and extremely efficient, and although basic, she cooked more than adequate fare for my needs. She had a rather old-fashioned outlook on life and position. I had on a couple of occasions asked her to call me Ella, but she'd refused.

"Oh, I couldn't possibly. There's a place for everything and everything in its place, as my mother always said. You are my employer, Miss Bridges, and it's only right I respect that," she'd insisted, so I'd let it be. Although it was an emotional wrench to be again addressed as 'Miss' when I had once been a wife.

Unfortunately there was one complication. She would not set foot in the pantry, and considering this was where the food was stored, it posed a bit of a dilemma. Of course it wasn't the pantry per se that was the problem; it was the secret dining room beyond and the spirit of a young woman currently stranded there that was the real issue.

A temporary solution had been to remove all the goods and store them in a large cupboard in the kitchen proper, which I'd done last Sunday on Mrs. Shaw's day off. I'd enlisted the help of my brother Jerry, who alongside his wife Ginny and her Godfather Sir Albert Montesford, Scotland Yard's current Police Commissioner, were the only people to know of my special gift.

While this solution pleased Mrs. Shaw, it didn't bring me any closer to solving the real mystery. Just who was the ghost in my dining room? How had she died? And more importantly, where were her remains? I was hoping the visit to the village later would shed more light on the matter. I was going to visit my friend Harriet Dinworthy, a published local historian and founder of the village library. I needed to find out more about my home.

CHAPTER THREE

A s I crossed the hall to the breakfast room in search of the coffee I knew Mrs. Shaw would have waiting, the telephone rang.

"Hello, Linhay 546."

"'Ello, do you get rid o' dogs?"

"I beg your pardon?" I said, taken aback. The accent was pure cockney and I had no idea who it was.

"I said, do you get rid o' dogs? I 'ave a problem. The missus finks I'm losin' me marbles, but I'm not, you know. Damn thing keeps movin' me slippers. Found 'em 'arf buried in the yard last night."

"I'm terribly sorry, but I think you have the wrong number."

"Ain't you the Paranormal Investigator then? Dog's bin dead for three months."

I knew then exactly who it was.

"Jerry, you absolute rotter!"

I waited patiently for Jerry to stop laughing. He had one of those almost silent laughs when highly amused, just a constant hiccupping wheeze that started in his chest and set his shoulders shaking. I could almost see him wiping his eyes with his handkerchief as the mirth took hold.

"Sorry, Ella, I couldn't resist. I've waited months to do that."

I knew to what he was referring. The previous Christmas holidays had been a lovely time spent with Ginny and Jerry in London. Jerry had gifted me with an exquisite brooch in the shape of a cat, made from black onyx with two small sapphires for eyes. But Ginny, with a flourish and a great deal of excitement, had presented me with a fine silver box of gilt-edged calling cards proclaiming me to be a Physic Investigator. I still didn't know if it had been a joke or not. They were now safely locked up in my writing desk drawer, never again to see the light of day.

"Do you forgive me?" Jerry said, catching his breath.

"I'll think about it," I replied, although I knew he'd hear the smile in my voice.

"Actually, I was hoping to come down and see you, if that's all right? I'm meeting with a chap on the island in a couple of hours. He has a motorcycle I might buy."

"Of course. I had thought I'd visit the library later, but it can wait until tomorrow."

"Jolly good. I'll see you about one o' clock then. Cheerio."

I replaced the receiver and rang for Mrs. Shaw, telling her my brother would be joining me for lunch.

Jerry's imminent arrival was announced by the tremendous roar of an engine coming up the lane. I hurriedly donned my coat and shoes and rushed out to meet him.

"Well, what do you think, Ella? She's a stunner, isn't she?" he enthused, dismounting and removing his goggles.

"Oh, she's terrific, Jerry!" I agreed as I circled the sleek-lined machine with its open-top sidecar, and admired the shiny black and silver paintwork.

"She's a 1930 BSA, so only five years old, and I got her for a song. And look here ... " Jerry crouched down, so I followed suit. "This is a Watsonian sidecar fitted on the company's quick-fit chassis, and with a simple flick of this lever here, the whole thing can be detached and stored until needed."

"How clever." I dutifully enthused. I knew nothing about motorcycles, but Jerry was obviously thrilled with his acquisition and I was very happy for him. "Where are you going to keep her?"

"Actually, I was wondering if I could keep her here until I can sort something out back in the city?"

"Absolutely. You can put her in the garage, seeing as though it's empty." One of the things I hadn't yet managed to do was learn to drive, although I planned on remedying that as soon as possible. Driving had been John's domain and I'd sold his car along with the house.

"So what's this?" I asked, pointing to a large curiously-shaped object precariously balanced in the sidecar.

"Oh, yes, I nearly forgot about that. It's a gift for you."

I watched as Jerry lifted the item out and stood it up. With a quick flick of his wrist worthy of a professional magician, the canvas was slung aside and there, resplendent in matching shiny black paint with a silver bell and a basket on the front, was a bicycle.

"Oh, Jerry, you bought me a bicycle, how wonderful."

"I thought it ideal for you to ride about the island on. There must be much of it you haven't seen yet and what better way than this?"

I smiled inwardly at Jerry's hope that I could explore the entire island on a bicycle. At its longest point it was eighteen miles, rather too much to do in one go, especially considering I hadn't ridden one since I was a child. But cycling to the village or the beach was wonderful idea.

"It's perfect, Jerry, thank you."

"So do you want to try her out then?"

"I'll say. But I'm a bit rusty."

"No need to worry, I'll be right behind you. Once you get back into it, you'll be racing along in no time. I say, do you have a matching pair of shoes inside just like those?"

I looked down and burst out laughing. In my haste I had inadvertently put on one black and one brown shoe. "As a matter of fact, I do. You never know, perhaps I'll start a new fashion craze."

Still laughing at my idiocy, I grasped the handle bars, perched myself on the seat and set off down the track lane at a snail's pace, and with a not inconsiderable wobble. I could hear Jerry jogging alongside shouting encouraging words, but before long I'd left him behind as I gained in confidence and it all came back to me.

It was exhilarating with the wind in my hair and the hedgerows rushing past. I felt I could go for miles. Unfortunately, Phantom had other ideas and suddenly materialised right before me in the road. I should have ridden through him, but in that split second the thought never entered my head and I swerved to avoid him. Of course the inevitable happened, I hit the grass bank, fell off and rolled down the slight incline into the ditch below, where Jerry found me sitting in an inch of dirty water and clutching my right wrist.

"Good god, Ella, are you all right? What on earth happened? You were doing so well."

"Phantom," I said, with no further explanation necessary.

"Come on, we need to get you home and the doctor called to take a look at that wrist."

So with Jerry wheeling my luckily undamaged bicycle back with one hand, and holding me up with the other, I limped back home. Mrs. Shaw immediately called Doctor Brookes, settled me in the drawing room with hot sweet tea, a roaring fire and instructions to ring the little bell she had placed on the side table should I require anything at all.

By the time the doctor arrived, I was feeling much better, although a little sore and my wrist was throbbing terribly. I'd managed a couple of bites of lunch, but couldn't stomach more without feeling nauseous. Luckily,

Jerry had no such appetite loss and managed both to polish off his own in short order, and finish mine.

Jerry was putting his motorcycle in the garage when Mrs. Shaw announced, "Doctor Brookes, Miss Bridges," and showed him in.

The doctor made an entrance that day which was rather shocking on two counts. Firstly, I had assumed him to be old, somewhat stooped and rather frail, so the exceptionally tall and handsome man with startling green eyes and dark red hair, which fell foppishly over his forehead, was unexpected to say the least and I was momentarily lost for words. However, my power of speech deserted me completely when he took a large stride into the room, tripped over nothing at all and ended up sprawled across the rug.

Mrs. Shaw, who was still hovering in the background, rushed forward in aid. "Good heavens, Doctor Brookes, are you all right?"

"Oh, I really am most awfully sorry," he said, staggering to his feet and revealing a bloody nose. "I was trying to avoid the cat."

"Cat?" said Mrs. Shaw in a confused tone. "We have no cat here, Doctor. You must have hit your head when you fell. Here, sit down and I'll bring you some hot sweet tea." And with that she rushed out.

She must have passed Jerry on the way as he entered not a moment later. "Good afternoon, Doctor, so what's the prognosis… oh, I say, what happened here then?"

At that point the doctor and I had not spoken a word to each other. I had yet to find my voice and with a handkerchief over half his face and watering eyes, Doctor Brookes was in no fit state. But Jerry's entrance broke the spell.

I rose. "The doctor has had a slight accident, Jerry. He tripped on his way in and as you can see has bloodied his nose. Perhaps you could show him to the cloakroom where he can clean himself up?" I suggested.

As they left, I frowned at the realisation the doctor had probably seen Phantom, but glancing around, could see no sign of him. Sitting back down, my foot connected with a small bottle of pills and I noticed Doctor Brookes' Gladstone bag lay open, partially disgorging its contents over my rug. I knelt and began to replace the various items, marvelling at the paraphernalia a medical man needed to lug around daily. Bandages, pills and powders lay alongside a prescription pad and a note. "PM police." I imagined a doctor would need to work closely with the police for all sorts of reasons, and resolved not to take up too much of his time if he had an appointment with them this evening. I'd finished tidying up when he and Jerry reappeared.

He looked much better. Gone were the streaming eyes and the blood, although a slight swelling and the beginnings of a bruise across the bridge of his nose were apparent. He sat opposite with a rueful smile. "Miss Bridges, I wonder if you'll allow me to start again. As you can see, I am more than capable of entering a room in a dignified manner. I am Nathaniel Brookes, the doctor on the island. I've recently taken over the practice from my father who has retired. Now, I understand that you have an injury to your wrist. Let's take a look, shall we?"

As he carefully and gently inspected my wrist, I took in the long tapered fingers with their short clean fingernails, and unbidden, the absence of a wedding ring. I frowned, cross with myself for being so ridiculous. Unfortunately, Doctor Brookes mistook my meaning.

"I'm sorry, am I hurting you?"

"No, not at all. I was thinking of something else entirely. Please continue."

"Well, the good news is it isn't broken. But it is badly sprained. I'll strap it up for you and give you something for the pain, but use it sparingly for a few days to allow it to heal. I'll come back in a week to see how you're getting on, but do call the surgery if you are having any problems and I'll come back sooner."

I thanked him, and as Mrs. Shaw showed him out, Jerry came to say goodbye.

"Are you sure you'll be all right, Ella? I feel pretty wretched about the whole thing."

"Of course I will, Jerry, it's only a sprain. I'll be right as rain in no time. And don't blame yourself. It was hardly your fault."

Accepting my reassurances, he gave me a quick peck on the cheek and, having elicited a promise that I'd call him if needed, he left to catch the train back to London.

Once again alone and having eaten very little at lunch, I ravenously ate the supper Mrs. Shaw had made and retired early. My plan for the next day was to go to the post office with the letters I had written that morning, and to visit the library. I still had some research to do.

CHAPTER FOUR

The next morning, I awoke to find the throbbing pain in my wrist had lessened to a dull ache, which thankfully became barely noticeable once I had taken the prescribed pain relief. After a breakfast of porridge followed by toast and fruit jam, all consumed with a splendid Assam tea courtesy of Ginny, I informed Mrs. Shaw I would be out for most of the morning, so to dispense with elevenses.

"Will you be requiring lunch, Miss Bridges?"

"Well, that rather depends on how long my visit to the library takes. If I find something of interest I could be gone some time."

"Well, in that case I will prepare a cold buffet lunch which won't spoil and will be ready upon your return. Would that suit?"

"A splendid idea, Mrs. Shaw, well done." And with that sorted out I set off for the village.

All small villages, regardless of their size or geographical location, are subject to gossip and hearsay. No one quite knows where the tales originate, but sooner or later the story has been passed along so many times it barely resembles the original at all. The village of Meadham on Linhay Island was no different, and the most recent rumour concerned the new-found love of Sir Robert Harlow. He was a retired city financier and current owner of Arundel Hall, the large manor house atop the bluff overlooking Smuggler's Cove. Apparently, after just one glance, he had become utterly smitten with American actress Patty-Mae Ludere, whom he had met at a ball at The Dorchester. Without further ado, he'd gone down on one knee in the middle of a packed dance floor and proposed marriage.

While I didn't know Sir Robert particularly well, the whole thing sounded preposterous. Our paths had crossed several times in the months I'd been living there and he'd always struck me as a highly intelligent, quietly spoken and mild-mannered gentleman. He was of middling years with hair more salt than pepper, and sported a full, but neatly trimmed beard and moustache a shade or two lighter than his hair. He was of average height, trim and fit, and habitually wore Harris Tweed.

It was therefore a complete shock when I reached the post office, saw what I thought was a stranger alight from his Rolls Royce dressed like a dandy, and realised it was Robert himself.

"Good morning, Miss Bridges, I trust you are well?" It was at that moment he spied the sling. "Oh, forgive me, I didn't realise you were injured. Nothing too serious, I hope?"

I shook my head. "No, just a silly sprain, that's all."

I was trying not to stare. Gone was the grey hair and beard which had given him a sophisticated air. Now he sported a slicked back hairstyle and a pencil-thin moustache, both of which had been poorly dyed to a rather patchy black. The Harris Tweed was nowhere in sight, in its place white flannel trousers and a powder-blue jacket topped by a navy and white polka dot cravat, and a matching handkerchief just visible in his top pocket. It was ludicrous attire for any man at this time of year, let alone one who lived here and should know better, giving no consideration to our inclement weather. It may have been early spring, but there was a cold snap in the air exacerbated by the wind coming off the sea. He must have been chilled to his marrow. I was trying to imagine what had wrought such an incongruous change when the passenger door of the Rolls opened and I had my answer.

A pair of silken-clad legs shod in the highest red heels I had ever seen emerged first, slowly followed by a mass of white fur crowned by a shock of platinum blonde hair. Calculating blue eyes beneath finely arched brows and thick black lashes appraised me, and dismissed me as no threat in an instant. She tottered quickly to Robert and linking a proprietary arm through his, simpered through lips as scarlet as her shoes, "Bobby, honey, aren't you going to introduce me?"

I flinched, as what I had expected to be dulcet tones rang out as a high-pitched, childish and exaggerated drawl.

"Of course, my dear. Miss Bridges, may I introduce Miss Ludere?"

"Oh, call me Patty-Mae, sugar, everyone does." She giggled, holding out her left hand as if expecting me to kiss it. But more probably to show off the ring on her engagement finger. Though I could hardly miss it, the diamond being of similar size to a sparrow's egg. So the rumour was true.

I smiled. "Of course, and I'm Ella. I'm sorry, I'm afraid I can't shake hands," I said, lifting my sling.

"Oh, now, don't you worry about that none. Where I come from friends hug, and I just know we're going to be friends."

And with that I was suddenly engulfed in a powdery perfumed embrace, and the air above each ear kissed melodramatically.

As she leaned back and let me go, I could see fine lines around her eyes and mouth, which the thick make-up couldn't quite disguise. I had initially thought us of similar age, but she was at least ten years my senior and probably more. Almost half Robert's age.

A polite clearing of the throat interrupted us.

"Patty-Mae, shouldn't we let Ella get on?"

"Oh, of course, silly me. But dear Ella, you must come up to The Hall and have dinner with us. Please do say you will."

Really what could I say? "Dinner sounds wonderful, thank you."

Then, as if the thought had suddenly occurred to her, she gushed, "I know, we'll have a proper dinner party to celebrate our engagement. What do you say, Bobby, isn't that the most wonderful idea?"

"If a small dinner party is what you want, Patty-Mae, then that is what you shall have. Now … "

"Oh, goody," she said, clapping her hands and bouncing on her heels. "I'll get on with it right away. Come on, Bobby. Goodbye, Miss Bridges, look out for the invitation." And with that she carefully sashayed her way to the car.

"Patty-Mae, I still need to pick up my letters."

"What? Oh, go ahead without me, honey, you know I can't stomach that nauseating little man," she said, casting a vicious look at the post office where I was sure the Post Master was spying on us. "I'll wait for you in the Rolls."

Robert turned to me and smiled. "I do hope we've not kept you, Ella."

"Not at all, Robert, I'm heading to the post office myself actually and then up to the library."

"Well, in that case, let me accompany you."

As we crossed the street I congratulated him on his engagement.

"Thank you, my dear. I'm a little long in the tooth, I know, but one rarely gets a second chance at love, especially with such a vibrant young creature as Patty-Mae. I thought it wise to grab her with both hands. Metaphorically speaking of course."

"Well, I wish you both much happiness," I said as he opened the door and we entered the post office.

There was only one post office on the island, and it was run by a tall, thin man with a weasel-like face. Cedric Tipping was a confirmed bachelor of middling years and, although he was always polite to the point of obsequiousness, perhaps uncharitably, I had never really taken to him. Perchance it was his small coal-black eyes, set unnaturally close together, that stared at you for a moment longer than was comfortable. Or the beak-like nose, which he constantly sniffed and wiped at with a crumpled and yellowing handkerchief, coupled with his stertorous breathing. Possibly it was the way he shook your hand in greeting, hanging on to it a little longer than necessary. Or perhaps it was his penchant for idle gossip.

"Good morning, good morning," said the Post Master. "Miss Bridges, I do hope you are on the mend after your bicycle accident yesterday?"

How had he found out so quickly?

"I hope this is a lesson you've learned. I always say if God had wanted us to ride bicycles, we would have been born with wheels." He chuckled, clearing his throat noisily and sniffing. "I was just saying to Mr. Phipps the greengrocer how I hoped the young doctor had prescribed plenty of bed-rest."

Well, the cheek of the man!

"It was nothing, Mr. Tipping, I assure you. A simple sprained wrist, that's all. I've done worse damage pruning my roses."

"And what did you think of the young doctor, my dear? I'm surprised he let you out and about after a nasty shock like that. I was saying to Mr. Wellington the chemist only last week how qualified doctors are getting younger and younger nowadays."

My retort died in my throat as he turned to address Robert.

"And how are you this fine morning, Sir Robert? You certainly have a spring in your step. New love must suit you." He tapped the side of his nose and winked a rheumy eye salaciously. Although to give him his due, he managed to cover his shock at Robert's new look admirably. "And may I be the first to congratulate you on your up-coming nuptials. Now here is your mail. I've bundled it up all neatly for you and taken the liberty of separating it into the many tradesman's bills, which of course are to be expected considering the work you've had done on The Hall, and general correspondence. Mostly quite ordinary, but two from the Americas, which I have put at the top. There's no need to thank me, Sir Robert, it's all part of the service."

I think I was the only one who noticed the tightening of Sir Robert's jaw as he took the proffered letters, but of course he was far too well-mannered to react. Although I had the feeling he'd like to bash Cedric over the head with his umbrella for his impertinence.

"Thank you, Tipping, most kind."

I smiled at the tactful way he'd taken the Post Master down a notch.

"Can I give you a lift, Ella? I'd like to discuss the dinner party with you," he said, turning to me.

"That would be most welcome, Robert, thank you." And with that, we abandoned Mr. Tipping, no doubt already devising ways to pass on the latest gossip.

We continued our discussion outside, both of us studiously ignoring Mr. Tipping, who all but had his ear pressed to the window.

"About this dinner party of Patty-Mae's, it will only be small, nothing too lavish you understand, but still I think it might be too much for my elderly housekeeper to deal with on her own and I wonder, do you know of anyone who might help until I can reorganise my staff?"

"Actually, Robert, I may know of someone," I said. I was of course thinking of my own Mrs. Shaw who I felt would not only be more than up to the task, considering her experience, but would welcome the opportunity to do more than serve simple meals for me. "However, I would have to ask her first."

"Of course. Here, let me give you my card. My telephone number is on there. Perhaps you could call and let me know? Now, let me drop you at the library."

My reason for visiting the library was to find out as much about my new home as I could. The discovery of the secret room had piqued my curiosity. However, I didn't expect to learn that Robert and I had more in common than I had thought, nor that there was a centuries-old curse attached to Arundel Hall. A curse which was about to make itself known in the most insidious of ways.

CHAPTER FIVE

The library was a new and very welcome addition to island life, and was housed in a large anteroom off the foyer of The Royal Norfolk Hotel on the seafront. An exceptionally grandiose arc-shaped building with magnificent views across the water. It was originally built in the reign of King George IV to cater to the wealthy elite and fashionable, who came to the island for its clean air, temperate summer climate, and to partake of the restorative salt baths. The interior of the hotel was still in its original, flamboyant Regency style, with the public rooms and private bedchambers decorated with Chinoiserie wallpaper of numerous colours. The foyer had a magnificent domed ceiling and everywhere you looked were elaborate chandeliers, decorative friezes and gilded furniture. It was opulence at its best and spoke of wealth and pleasures of a bygone era. It still attracted the well-heeled and affluent all year round, which did much to help the island's economy.

Harriet was the dearest old soul who, although in her early sixties, had a mind as sharp as a tack and the energy of someone half her age. Both an islander and a retired historian, she was ideally placed to help me in my quest. For what Harriet didn't know about the island really wasn't worth knowing. Jerry, Ginny, and I had been present at the grand opening of the library a few months ago, as had Robert, and once Harriet realised I was not only new to the island, but living alone, she had practically adopted me. She insisted on addressing me by my given name as persons of that generation are wont to do, and greeted me like the granddaughter she had never had.

"Isobella, my dear child, how lovely to see you," she said, giving me a hug and a light, powdery kiss on my cheek. Then she spied my companion and her face turned pale.

"Good god, Robert, is that you?"

Robert spluttered and I watched a crimson blush suffuse his neck and tinge his face. "Of course it's me, Hettie, who else did you think it was?" he said gruffly, while I frowned at the name 'Hettie'. I'd never heard Harriet addressed as such before.

Heels beat a staccato over the marble floor to join us "Well, I declare! Would you look at this place," Patty-Mae said with eyes as big as saucers. "If that don't beat all. Bobby honey, we should decorate the hall just like this, don't you think?"

Robert sighed and patted her hand. "We'll see, Patty-Mae, we'll see. Now let me introduce Harriet Dinworthy, author and local historian, and of course the founder of this wonderful library. Harriet, this is Patty-Mae Ludere."

"His fiancée," Patty-Mae added, holding out her hand to show off the ring. "It's just so lovely to meet Robert's old friends."

I cringed as Harriet blanched. Had she emphasised the word old? Surely not.

"And you simply must come to our supper party, Harriet. Shouldn't she, Robert?"

"Dinner, Patty-Mae. We have dinner here, remember?"

Patty-Mae giggled. "Bless your heart, Bobby, why I do believe I'd forget my own head if it wasn't fastened on."

Robert turned back to Harriet. "It's just a small gathering of close friends. You'd be most welcome."

However, before Harriet could answer, Patty-Mae clapped in delight. "That's settled then. How excitin'. We'll see you both very soon and don't forget to dress up. Come along, honey." And with that she took Robert's arm and practically dragged him to the car.

Harriet and I stood silently in the foyer of the hotel and watched them leave. I think we were both at a loss for words. Patty-Mae Ludere was a force of nature, garrulous, loud, over the top and obviously used to getting her own way, but there was something else I couldn't put my finger on. Perhaps it was simply the fact we weren't used to such flamboyance and over-familiarity in our quiet English village.

"Have you known Robert long, Harriet?" I asked eventually.

"All my life, dear," she said sadly, turning away. But not before I had seen the shimmering in her eyes.

"Silly old fool," she muttered.

I wasn't sure if she meant Robert or herself.

As we entered the library proper, Harriet seemed to mentally shrug off her previous mood and was back to being the friend I knew.

"I've been helping with some of the history of The Hall recently and I've found some interesting connections to your cottage. Oh, good heavens, what on Earth happened to your arm, Isobella?"

"Actually, I'm surprised you don't already know," I said. "Cedric Tipping knew almost every detail and it only happened yesterday afternoon. Jerry brought me a bicycle as a gift and I fell off. It's just a sprain, nothing to worry about."

"Oh, take no notice of Cedric Tipping, Isobella. That man is enough to try the patience of a saint. He has nothing better to do than gossip. He lives a very small life and is of the opinion he is a large fish in a small pond when nothing could be further from the truth. Personally I have very little time for the Cedric Tippings of this world. You'll find, when you reach my age, my dear, you have less and less tolerance of imbeciles and the fatuous. Now, let us not waste any more time talking about the asinine, we have far more interesting things to discuss."

I was rather taken aback at Harriet's rancorous tone. It was most unlike her, I thought, as I trailed on her heels.

She steered me to one of the many snug seating areas that were dotted around the library. As expected, the style was Regency with gold and green-striped fabric adorning the rosewood armchairs, and oriental rugs on the floor. The mahogany bookshelves rose to the ceiling on all walls, with some set perpendicular to provide intimate corners for reading or research and a large chandelier dominating the ceiling, its crystal teardrops glittering as they caught the light from outside. Dotted throughout were gilt and porcelain table lamps casting cosy glows over objets d'art, and it reminded me of one of the exclusive London clubs of which Jerry spoke.

Tea had already been laid by one of the hotel staff, along with roast beef sandwiches and a rather sumptuous watercress salad.

"One of the perks of being part of the hotel," Harriet said, with an uncharacteristic wink, her previous outburst forgotten.

Later, as a waitress cleared away the remaining detritus, Harriet spread out a large old map of the island.

"This is one of the maps I hunted down and procured whilst doing research for Robert. It dates from the latter half of the 1700s and as you can see, it clearly shows The Hall, and both St. Peter's and St. Mary's churches, both of which pre-date The Hall by several centuries. The island in its entirety at that time was owned by the Duke of Norfolk, who commissioned the building of Arundel Hall as a gift to his new young wife. But what's most interesting for you is this building here."

Harriet pointed out a block denoting a building on a very familiar part of the island.

"That's the cottage," I said.

"Indeed it is, but more importantly it was the Dower House."

"You mean it was the home of the Duke's mother?" I asked, astonished.

"Precisely, my dear. As you are no doubt aware, tradition dictated the widowed dowager moved out of the larger family residence once her son married, and I believe your cottage was specifically built for that purpose."

"Goodness, I had no idea my home had such a stately provenance. Although I am at a loss as to why it's known as a cottage. Isn't it a bit large?"

"I think we can safely assume it was a term of affection used to describe the smaller of the two properties. The Hall has eighteen bedrooms, two libraries, a saloon, a smoking room, a dining room and several others. Not to mention the servants' quarters and the kitchens. So anything with only the four bedchambers, a dining room and two reception rooms, plus of course the kitchen and staff quarters such as yours, would almost certainly be looked upon as a cottage."

"Harriet, this is absolutely fascinating. I can't thank you enough for your help."

"Oh, my dear girl, it's an absolute pleasure. But did I say I had finished?"

I laughed. "You mean there's more?"

"Of course there's more. I never leave a job unfinished, Isobella," she said, reaching for another map. "Now this map is nearly one hundred years later, a mere sixty years ago, and you'll see the landscape has changed considerably."

As she was pointing out some of the differences, several of the hotel guests wandered in to peruse the books.

"Do excuse me, my dear, duty calls. But when I return I'll tell you about the curse of The Hall."

A curse? Gosh, that sounded ominous.

As Harriet attended to her customers, I studied the map in more detail. The most obvious change was that the land belonging to the Arundel estate had diminished considerably and I made a note to ask Harriet about it. I saw the fishermen's cottages and the hotel, which I was currently sitting in, had both been added, along with numerous farmhouses and their lands and other larger residences. The village had grown considerably and was now easily recognisable. Both of the churches remained and were in fact still in use today. I decided I must visit them as soon as time allowed. The oyster beds and the brick field were likewise shown. I also noticed something much more interesting to me personally, the marking of a large area to the south of the cottage. So intent was I on my study that I didn't notice Harriet had returned.

"How are you getting on, my dear?"

"Oh, Harriet, you made me jump. I was completely lost in the map."

"We'll make an historian of you yet, Isobella." She laughed. "Do you have any questions?"

"Yes, a couple. I was intrigued about the acreage belonging to the Arundel estate. There have been some significant changes and I wondered why they would have had to sell off the land?"

"You're very observant, well spotted. Actually, that's partly to do with the curse I mentioned earlier. Here, let me ring for more tea then I'll close for a while so we're not interrupted."

Once the tea had arrived and the doors were locked, I settled back while Harriet told me about the curse.

"You see, Arundel Hall has been plagued with ill luck for the male owners and their spouses since the last stone was laid. The commissioning owner, the Eleventh Duke of Norfolk, built the hall for his first wife Marion. Sadly she died in childbirth not a year later. It was reported they were very much in love and the Duke never really got over her death."

"How very sad. What happened to the child?"

"Well, historical accounts are rather vague about the babe, but it's widely believed he was still-born, a double tragedy for the Duke. Then not quite four years later, he married a young woman called Frances, the daughter of the Duchess of Beaufort, who herself was a woman of questionable repute. Not many years into the childless marriage, Frances, who was described as being both delicate and irrational, became insane and was locked away for the rest of her life."

"Oh, how awful, Harriet! So he lost two wives?"

"Actually it was three, my dear. After a string of mistresses, the Duke, who was now into middle age, decided it was time to marry again. Frances had died several months earlier so he was free to take another spouse, and although he had a string of illegitimate offspring, he had yet to provide a legitimate heir. So for the final time the Duke got married. His third wife, Mary Ann, was much younger than he … " Harriet stopped and flashed a frown at the door.

"Harriet, what is it?" I asked, laying my hand on her arm when she failed to reply.

"Mmmm? Oh nothing, my dear. Something just occurred to me. Now where was I? Ah yes, Mary Ann was very popular and attractive and within a year had borne him a son. But not all was harmonious behind closed doors. The Duke, constantly usurped by his pretty and highly regarded wife, became surly and withdrawn. He forbade visitors and by the same token prohibited her from visiting friends. By all accounts, he had also restricted her time with her son. He spent much time with the boy himself and I posit he was sowing seeds of ill in the boy's mind against his mother. For a young woman in the prime of life who loved her child, relished company and was a gay and congenial hostess, this was a terrible hardship and before long the inevitable happened. She found solace in the arms of another."

My hands involuntarily flew to my mouth. "Oh no, who? What happened? Did the Duke find out?"

"I'm afraid he did. Her lover was his own stable master. Although accounts at the time differ slightly, the general consensus was that he was enraged beyond belief. So much so that he immediately went to his gun cabinet, took out the largest shotgun he could find and threatened to blow them both to kingdom come where they stood."

I gasped. "He killed them?"

"I don't think so. He may have been a bitter, selfish old man, but I find it hard to believe he was a cold-blooded murderer. Besides the ruckus had brought every available servant out to gawk and I doubt he wanted quite so many witnesses." She smiled wryly.

"So what happened?"

"No one knows. Mary Ann and her lover simply disappeared and were never seen nor heard from again. It's thought he banished them both, had the marriage annulled and cut her out of his will. He left everything to their son."

"So, do you think she lived a long and happy life together with her lover?" I asked.

Harriet shook her head. "I sincerely doubt it. The Eleventh Duke wasn't given to acts of benevolence as far as his last wife was concerned, and certainly not after such a public indignity. They didn't treat wifely infidelity lightly in those days and he would have been perfectly within his rights to have had her flogged. If it were a simple banishment then I would say they got away with it. But of course we'll never really know."

"But what of the curse?" I asked.

"Well, within days of his wife disappearing, the Duke sold Arundel Hall to one of his contemporaries. The only thing he took was his son. Everything else, right down to the silver buckles on his shoes, was left. The language of the time was rather convoluted so I'll take a few liberties with the translation, but in essence he was heard to yell as he mounted his horse," Harriet closed her eyes and recited from memory … "Beware all ye masters with mistresses who reside in this damnable place, for I curse it with my every breath. Never will the light of joy penetrate these accursed walls for here shall only live despondency and despair. Tragedy and misfortune will plague your days and your wives will be as harlots and she-devils. Until the last stone remains … "

"Harriet, that's truly appalling. What a horrible old man."

"Indeed he was. Never having been happy there himself and with far more than his share of tragedy and ill-luck, he was determined no other would be at peace within its walls."

"But do you believe it to be true?" I asked. "What happened to the owners who followed, were they struck down as the Duke said?"

Harriet laughed. "It's rather a conundrum, Isobella, and one I've mulled over for years. On the one hand I'm an historian, and as such look at the facts before me and the findings I unearth in my research to form a basis of truth as to what happened. Naturally not every question is answerable. We can only take educated guesses in some instances, but again they are based on the evidence before us. With regard to the curse, I can't honestly say whether I believe it or not. It all sounds too far-fetched to be real, but I find I can't dismiss so lightly what happened to the hall's subsequent owners."

"Oh, Harriet, do tell," I begged. I'd become enraptured with the whole tale and simply had to know what happened next.

Harriet removed her pince-nez and rubbed her eyes. Glancing at the ormolu clock above the fireplace, I realised I'd taken up far more of her time than I'd intended.

I began to rise. "Harriet, I'm so sorry. I didn't realise the time."

She waved her hand dismissively. "Oh, do sit down, Isobella, I'm not ready to be put out to pasture yet. There's not much more to tell anyway, just a rather potted history of ownership." She replaced her glasses and continued.

"The Eleventh Duke sold The Hall in 1807 to Baron Shelley who had coveted the place since its inception. He and his wife were of similar age, with children grown and gone. Elizabeth Shelley was reluctant to inhabit such a large property when they were both in their dotage and alone, but the Baron insisted, it was a contentious issue and caused much antagonism between them. As the years passed, they grew more and more distant, eventually living separate lives albeit in the same residence. Seven years after moving in, Elizabeth Shelley died in misery and unhappiness, and the Baron, riddled with guilt, took his own life."

"So the curse continued," I said, more to myself than Harriet. "Who came next?"

"Baron Shelley left The Hall to his eldest son Timothy, who took up residence with his wife Helen and two teenage daughters. At first they were happy at The Hall and two months later, to their utter surprise, they found out

Helen was with child. This was extremely unusual considering Helen was almost thirty-five years of age at the time, but they both took it as a good omen, especially when seven months later she gave birth to a boy, Algernon."

I put my head in my hands. "Something awful happened to him, didn't it?"

Harriet sighed and patted my knee. "Isobella, dear, are you sure you want to hear this?"

I nodded. "Of course. I'm fine, Harriet, really. It all happened so many years ago and there's nothing I can do about it. It just grieves me when it's children, I suppose."

Harriet looked at me for a little while longer then, apparently happy I wasn't going to break down, carried on.

"Well, of course you're quite right. Poor little Algernon died at just eight months old. There was nothing to indicate foul play and a cause was never found. The doctor who was summoned put it down as an accidental death. The loss of the boy tore the family apart and Helen eventually ran with her daughters in tow back to her parental home. But she was never the same after that, prone to long periods of melancholy and with no interest in life. She passed away a couple of years later. Timothy, with the loss of everything he held dear, remained at The Hall, but drowned his sorrows in a bottle. By all accounts, the times he was sober were rare and one evening, three or four years after the death of his son, a gang of armed robbers infiltrated his home intent on stealing the valuables. In a drunken rage he tried to defend himself, but obviously he was not in full control and was killed by a shotgun blast through the heart. During the years of his insobriety, he had lost all interest in his business and the running of the estate, so when it came to sorting out his affairs, it was found he died in extreme debt and was declared bankrupt. To pay off his debtors The Hall was put on the market, but it failed to find a buyer at first."

"Perhaps word of the curse had spread?" I said.

"Perhaps," Harriet agreed. "But in order to alleviate the demands of those Timothy Shelley was indebted to, some of the land was sold to raise money."

"Oh, so that's why there's such a change in the two maps you showed me."

"Precisely, and it also happened again with the pen-ultimate owner. However, there was one more who came first. In 1830, ten years after Timothy Shelley died, with much of the place shut up and the remainder looked after by a skeleton staff of three, The Hall changed hands once again. Now this is the one I find most interesting. See if you come to the same conclusion I did."

"Heavens, that sounds intriguing. I hope I can live up to your expectation, Harriet."

She laughed. "George Barnstaple was a naturalist and ornithologist. As you know, the bird life here is remark-able. Even today, in fact, in the spring, you can barely move without bumping into a twitcher. I've found them picnicking on my lawns and sat in my apple trees before now. But I digress. Back to George. He already had several published works under his belt which he'd also illustrated beautifully—I have copies here if you're interested—and The Hall was the most natural place for him to live and continue his work. He lived a quiet and solitary life and for almost four decades lived happily at The Hall until his death in 1871 at the grand old age of eighty-four."

"So the curse had been broken?" I paused and frowned. "No, that can't be right. Why would it have been? Wait a minute, you didn't mention his family. He was a bachelor, wasn't he, so the curse wouldn't have affected him?"

Harriet peered over her pince-nez, eyes shining as though I were a recalcitrant child who'd suddenly learned obedience.

"I knew you wouldn't fail me, Isobella. Sharp as a tack. You're quite correct."

"Well, surely that lends credibility to the authenticity of the curse?"

Harriet nodded. "It does seem that way, doesn't it? But as I said before, Isobella, I'm in two minds about it. It just seems too fantastical."

"I suppose you're right," I said, although I suspected if she knew I could see ghosts and had a phantom cat as a companion, she might have changed her mind. "So what happened next?"

"Well, with no family to bequeath The Hall to, Barnstaple stated in his will it should be sold to raise funds for the newly-founded Royal Society for the Protection of Birds. So once again it was on the market."

"Did it sell quite quickly this time?" I asked. "I would imagine the tales of the curse had somewhat diminished over the forty years George Barnstaple was the owner."

"I think you're most likely correct," Harriet agreed, "for The Hall was snapped up almost immediately. Although the difference this time was the new proprietor didn't reside in it full time. In fact he barely set foot in the place for years as he already owned a Georgian Manor house in London's Clapham Common and an apartment in Mayfair."

"He must have been wealthy. Was he a peer of the realm too?" I asked.

"Good heavens no! Far from it. Adam Worthington was a thoroughly nasty piece of work and had made his vast wealth through illicit gambling, robberies and prostitution. He practically ran London in those days, but he would get his just deserts when he moved to Arundel Hall."

"And this is the man Robert bought it from?"

"Not exactly. Robert and I aren't *that* ancient, you know. Robert was the next owner of course, but by then The Hall had once again remained empty for some time and needed finance to make it habitable."

I nodded. Most of the island knew Robert had been refurbishing Arundel for his retirement.

"So what happened to this villain?"

"Worthington was a wanted man, not just here, but in America. Scotland Yard and the Pinkerton Detective Agency had corresponded and determined the man was suspected of numerous crimes in both countries. But he remained elusive and he was very clever. None of the evidence gathered pointed to him directly, but they were sure he was the mastermind. When word reached him that they were getting close, he did a midnight flit and absconded to The Hall. He'd bought the place under another name, Henry Raymond. He changed his appearance and lived the life of a wealthy country gentleman for some time while the danger passed. But of course the lure of his former world was eventually too strong to resist. He missed the danger and excitement, the wheeling and dealing of his corrupt existence, but most of all he missed the company."

"Oh, so he'd moved to The Hall on his own? How long was he there?"

"Alone, you mean?" Harriet asked.

I nodded.

"Just shy of two years. Ah, I see what you're getting at. Well thought out, Isobella, I must admit the significance had eluded me. Well, it all changed when he moved not only his wife and children in, but his mistress and her youngsters too."

I cringed in disgust. How could anyone live like that?

"I know. Shocking, isn't it?" said Harriet, reading my mind. "But that wasn't all. Over a short period of time, so as not to raise the alarm in London, he moved in most of his gang and their partners and a life of drunken de-bauchery began. Gambling parties were rife in those days and of course women of dubious morals were already in residence. It was only a matter of time before the curse made itself known.

"The first body, that of a young prostitute, was found hanging from the chandelier in the foyer; the second, a minor henchman of Worthington's, was found drowned in an upstairs bathtub with his wrists cut. They were both thought to be suicide, but of course no one really knows. The only eye-witness was a young street girl who confessed to the goings-on at The Hall on her deathbed many years later. The bodies were disposed of and the remains never found. As the months went on, the body count rose, fights broke out among the inhabitants, many of which ended in death. The costs were also spiralling out of control and Worthington was forced to sell off considerable chunks of the estate to raise funds."

"Harriet, this is absolutely ghastly. It must have been harrowing for the children."

"And thereby hangs the sorriest tale of all, I'm afraid. The wife and mistress, who incidentally had lived quite happily in the knowledge of each other in the city, became incensed with jealousy and rage. The theory is they both simply went insane simultaneously and killed the other's children before turning the guns on themselves."

I found I couldn't speak. I couldn't imagine this horror, but Harriet hadn't finished.

"In abject despair and mad with grief, Adam Worthington ran from the house, screaming, and threw himself off the bluff onto the rocks of Smuggler's Cove below. He died instantly. The remaining members of his household fled and were never seen nor heard from again. The body known as that of Henry Raymond was taken to London and there his true identity as Adam Worthington was discovered. His will stipulated his estate was to be left to his children, but as they were all dead, the responsibility of disposal reverted to the state.

"By now, of course, the whole of the country had heard the tale. There wasn't a newspaper in circulation that wasn't running the story on its front page. Consequently, no one wanted anything to do with the place. Of course there were the usual thrill seekers and ghouls who came on day trips by the coach load to stand and peer through the iron gates, but there were no offers to purchase, even at a considerably reduced market value. So the place was once more closed and languished in decay until Robert came along.

"So there you have it, my dear, the rather insalubrious history of Arundel Hall and its dreadful curse."

I thanked Harriet for her time.

"Not quite what you were expecting, my dear?"

I shook my head. No doubt I would be plagued by nightmares later.

CHAPTER SIX

I awoke the next morning to a light tap on my door. "Come in," I said, groggily sitting up and reaching for my bed jacket.

My eyes were gritty and my head pounded horribly. I had been right about the nightmares. On my return home I'd found the promised cold buffet laid out and had taken a tray to the cosy sitting room in front of the fire. I'd sat long into the night, nursing my second medicinal brandy while I pondered the tale of the curse. Eventually, in the small hours, I'd wearily climbed the stairs and fallen into a disturbed sleep. Now it was apparently morning and I felt as though I hadn't slept at all.

Mrs. Shaw came in, balancing my breakfast tray, and deftly set it up on the counterpane. A glance to the pillow next to me showed Phantom curled in a ball, fast asleep.

"Thank you, Mrs. Shaw. What time is it?"

"A quarter after nine. I thought it was unusually late for you, so took the liberty of making your breakfast."

"Of course, that's fine, Mrs. Shaw. I had rather a disturbed sleep. Tell me, have you heard of the curse of Arundel Hall?" I asked while I buttered my toast and took the top off my egg.

"A curse on the big house on the bluff? No, I can't say I have. What's it all about then?"

I proceeded to tell her, very briefly, of the first owner cursing The Hall for its subsequent inhabitants.

"Oh, a Romany, was he?"

I started. "No, I don't think so, why?"

"Well, I'd imagine you'd have to have some knowledge and skill. I doubt any Tom, Dick, or Harry could do something like that, not that I believe such nonsense, of course. Will there be anything else?"

"There is one other thing, Mrs. Shaw. Sir Robert approached me yesterday about some additional help for his housekeeper for a small dinner party. I naturally thought of you, but said I would have to ask you first."

"A dinner party? Me? Oh well, I'm not sure I'm the one to ask, I . . . "

Good heavens, was the woman flustered?

"Oh, come now, Mrs. Shaw. I'm led to believe it will be a very modest group, myself included, so nothing too complicated."

"Well, I'm a little out of practice so . . . "

Out of practice? She'd only been with me a short time. I couldn't fathom her reticence.

I smiled to take the command from my next words.

"Mrs. Shaw, this is no time for false modesty. with your excellent credentials and experience, I'm sure this will prove to be effortless for you. You would in fact be doing me a favour as well as Sir Robert. I'd like you to help."

I watched as her back straightened and her chin rose. Her eyes fixed on a position above my head. "Well, if you put it like that. I know Mrs. Butterworth marginally. We attend the same church. I'll see to it. Is that all?" she asked stiffly.

"It is, Mrs. Shaw, and thank you."

Well, what on Earth was that all about? I thought as she left. Admittedly, I hadn't known Mrs. Shaw long, but flustered was not a state I'd thought her capable of. Brusque, no nonsense, and decisive perhaps, but flustered? Never. I'd obviously caught her by surprise. I shrugged, dismissing the incident, and continued with my breakfast while I pondered on how a Duke would have the skills to put such a strong curse on a building. *I must ask Harriet about it,* I thought. Then realised I'd forgotten to ask her my second question while at the library. I felt I really must start writing things down and vowed to purchase a small notebook at the earliest opportunity.

Once dressed, I ventured downstairs and was just passing the hall telephone when it rang. Expecting Jerry and another of his practical jokes, I was surprised when I heard Harriet's voice.

"Good morning, dear, how did you sleep?"

I confessed I'd had a disturbed night and was still feeling a little sluggish.

"Well, I'm sure it won't last, dear, but I have several recipes for aiding sleep. I'll send Giles over with them."

The elderly Giles was Harriet's titular butler and chauffeur, and although I had never spoken with him, I knew him by sight.

"That's very kind of you, Harriet. Incidentally, I asked Mrs. Shaw earlier if she'd heard about the curse. She said she hadn't, but made rather a good point. Wouldn't the Duke have had to have some sort of training in order to cast such a curse? She wondered if there were Romany involved. Do you know?"

"I certainly don't know about any training, but the Romany had camps all over the island in those days, so he may very well have come into contact with them. Or he may have sought them out with the purpose of learning such a skill. It's not something I can verify of course."

"No, of course not, but it does answer the question. Now is there something I can help you with?"

"Actually, I remembered you wanted to ask me something else yesterday. Was it about the boundary marking near your cottage by any chance?"

"Yes, it was. I only remembered myself this morning. Do you know what it is?"

"I believe you'll find it's a walled garden. They were very popular in Victoria's time and I suspect yours was added then."

"Harriet, why that's simply marvellous news. I do so love my garden and it's been in the back of my mind to add a produce section. But if one's already in place, it will save a huge amount of work."

"I'm so glad I've cheered you, Isobella. I was feeling rather guilty about the horrors I inflicted on you yesterday. I take it there's no sign of the wall then?"

"No, none at all. I don't think the garden has been seen to in a long time. There's a veritable forest of briars, hawthorn and weeds over that side, most of it way over my head. It will probably take an army to clear it all."

"Well, I don't have an army to hand, but I do know of a strong young man looking for work. He's not what you'd expect, but he's surprisingly knowledgeable about plants and a hard worker to boot."

"Send him over, Harriet, by all means. A gardener is exactly what I need."

Mrs. Shaw appeared just as I was replacing the receiver. Dressed in her coat and hat and with her handbag over one arm, she put on her gloves and asked, "I'm just popping down to the village, Miss Bridges. Is there anything you need?"

"Yes, a small notebook if you'd be so kind, Mrs. Shaw."

"Of course. I'll pick one up at the stationer's on my way past. Which reminds me, the post arrived earlier. I've left it on the hall table for you."

While Mrs. Shaw was out, I intended once again to visit the secret room, which I'd found behind the pantry. "Oh, Ella!" I chided myself in exasperation. I'd forgotten to tell Harriet about it. It had been my one reason for seeking her out in the first place, but with all the excitement of the curse it had slipped my mind. Thank goodness I'd remembered to ask for a notebook.

The postman had only delivered one item. The envelope was of impeccable quality with a gilt trim and I knew what it was before I even opened it: the invitation to dinner at Arundel Hall. I sighed and put it on the mantelshelf in the sitting room and, crossing to my desk, made a note to purchase a suitable engagement present. Absently, I noticed I had yet to look at the recent puzzle from Aunt Margaret, but before I could there was a knock at the door.

"Doctor Brookes, what a pleasant surprise."

"Good morning, Miss Bridges. I had a couple of home visits nearby and thought I'd come and check how your wrist is. I hope I'm not intruding?"

"No, not at all, do come in."

"I see you've dispensed with the sling," he said as I showed him into the sitting room.

I sat as he unwrapped the bandage.

"Well, it seems to be healing nicely. I'd advise keeping the support on for a few days, but no more than that. Try not to overuse it for a week or so afterward and it should be back to full strength in no time."

As he rose, his eye caught sight of the invitation. "Ah, I see you've been invited up to The Hall. We received our invitation this morning too."

We? I thought dismally. I'd been under the impression the doctor was single. Had rather hoped he was, I admitted to myself with some surprise.

"Do you know Robert and Patty-Mae well?" I asked.

"Him well enough. Her I don't know at all," he added sharply. "Robert's more my father's friend than mine.

He's been the family physician for years. Unfortunately, father's a bit under the weather at the moment so I'll have to attend alone. Unless…" Bright green eyes looked at me from under a fringe of dark red hair. "Would it be awfully improper of me to ask to be your escort for the evening?"

I stood and couldn't help the huge smile. "Not at all. I'd like that very much, Doctor Brookes."

His smile mirrored my own. "Well, in that case I'm sure we can dispense with the formalities. Nathaniel," he said, holding out his left hand in deference to my injured right one.

"Ella," I replied, and shook it.

"I'll pick you up at seven then?"

I nodded. Perhaps the evening would turn out to be pleasant after all.

CHAPTER SEVEN

The knocking of my heels on the bare stone treads echoed as I descended the servants' stairs to the kitchen, and I thought what a ludicrous position it was for a dining room. How could guests be expected to traverse this gloom, then proceed through the staff kitchen and then through the pantry to eat? I could just imagine titled ladies in their finery having to negotiate this narrow space, their gowns catching on the rough plaster, ruining cloth and stitching. No, that would never work. The door I had found must be for staff access only, which meant there must be another way leading from the main house which I hadn't yet found. As I mentally went through the positions of the rooms on the primary floor and the likelihood of another secret panel, I reached the pantry where Phantom was already waiting for me.

"Phantom, if it's not too much trouble, I really could do with some help."

He pinned me with a disdainful look for an instant, then disappeared through the solid door to the room beyond. I sighed and, crouching down, clicked the latch to release the door, then followed him in.

Once I'd lit the new candles in the wall sconces, I sat in the carver at the top end of the large rectangular table and looked around. This room never failed to take my breath away. It was simply stunning. My first impression upon discovery had been one of austerity and gloom, particularly as there was no natural light. Ginny had found the place quite chilling, but the more I ventured down here, the more I appreciated the detail and workmanship. I'd spent a lot of time in the interim period cleaning the place up, prior to hiring Mrs. Shaw.

The artistry of the oak wall panels was exquisite, and it was obvious master craftsmen had been employed to produce them. From the ceiling down to the middle was quite plain, but the lower half was sculpted into something that looked like draped cloth, which I had subsequently found out was called linenfold. Along the wide rail, which split the two halves, a row of acorns chased each other around the room, but it was the highly decorated ceiling I found most enchanting. Each panel was intricately carved with vines and interspersed throughout were rosebuds and roses, not stylised ones like the Tudor version, but realistic replicas in various stages of bloom. It was like a garden. I couldn't wait to hold my first dinner party here and had already imagined how festive it would look at Christmas.

But first there was the matter of the unfortunate resident to deal with.

As though she'd heard my thoughts, the woman rose from her place in the fireside chair and began to float gently back and forth. Unlike Phantom, she hadn't acquired any form of solidity, and I could clearly see the fireplace through her elaborate gown. It was aqua in colour with a full length hooped skirt and adorned with lace and bows at her cleavage, and the end of the elbow length sleeves. Her dark hair was piled high and topped off with an elaborate feather ensemble. At her throat were three strings of pearls, which matched the bracelet and earrings, and on the third finger of her left hand was a ring with a large central pearl, surrounded by garnets. Whoever she was, she'd obviously had wealth.

I don't know how long I sat there contemplating my next move, but I was suddenly shaken back to the present by the slam of a motorcar door. Mrs. Shaw! I quickly ran to the pantry and saw her wave at Harriet's driver Giles. I don't know what possessed me to do what I did next, I ran back into the dining room clicked the door in place and leaned back against it with a sigh. Then it struck me: I was trapped.

I could faintly hear Mrs. Shaw bustling about in the kitchen unpacking groceries and humming to herself. It looked as though I would be stuck for a while. I glanced at the far end of the room and saw Phantom's tail disappear through the wall.

"I'm sure you do that on purpose knowing I can't follow," I hissed.

To my surprise he came back through and sat down.

Well, I suppose it was as good a time as any to explore, so taking a candle I began to study the panel where Phantom had once again vanished. As I moved to the far corner I gasped as the flame began to flicker. There was a draft coming through, so there must be a space behind. The panel was so snug against its neighbours there wasn't even the tiniest join to signal a disguised door. I worked my way around it, carefully applying pressure, but there was nothing. Thinking it may work in the same way as the pantry door I rested the candle on the parquet floor, and on hands and knees looked for a hidden latch, but again was disappointed. There was absolutely nothing there. So whatever triggered the opening had to be somewhere else in the room, but where to start?

I tried to think about it logically. Phantom disappeared through a panel which, upon further investigation, due to the flickering candle flame, indicated a likely cavity behind, but there was no apparent way of opening it. The only other unusual aspect to the room was the ghost. I stopped to think. Since I'd first discovered her here, the woman had never ventured away from the fireplace, "Could it really be that simple?" I said aloud.

Approaching, I began to study the ornate marble. The design mirrored that of the ceiling with vines and roses across the frontage, but the sides were made up of statuary in the form of animals. Small birds sat in branches above while a fox sat at floor level on the left side and a hare at the right. After what seemed like hours of pushing and pulling every little carving, on the top left, I discovered a rosebud raised slightly higher than others. With a deep breath I pushed and was rewarded by a click behind me. Turning, I saw the panel had swung forward an inch. I'd found the secret door.

I slowly approached and, holding the candle aloft, carefully pulled the panel toward me. I let out an involuntary cry and stumbled back in shock for there, at the foot of a stone staircase, was a broken skeleton.

CHAPTER EIGHT

"Hello, who's there?" I heard Mrs. Shaw shout faintly from the kitchen.

Ignoring her for the moment, I took a step forward and looked in more detail at the pile of bones. Loosely wrapped around the top vertebrae were three strands of pearls, one had broken and a few loose gems were scattered about. The wrist was likewise adorned, and laying on the stone flags were a pair of pearl earrings. The pearl and garnet ring lay loosely encircled on the third finger of the left hand and tatty scraps of once blue fabric, rotted with time, clung to the bones like moss on damp rocks. I'd finally found the body of my spectral guest. Now all I had to do was identify her.

I strode over to the door and let myself out through the pantry, where I was saved by my quick instincts from being knocked senseless by Mrs. Shaw brandishing a frying pan.

"Now, Mrs. Shaw, please calm yourself. There's nothing to panic about."

"Miss Bridges, really! You frightened me to death. Where on Earth did you come from?"

"From the pantry, Mrs. Shaw. There's a room behind there and I'm afraid I've made a rather gruesome discovery. It's…"

"I knew there was something wrong in there, didn't I tell you? What have you found?"

There really wasn't a delicate way of telling her. "I'm afraid it's a body. Well, a skeleton to be exact. It's obviously been there a long time."

I'd expected her to fall apart, but the opposite happened. She took control immediately. What an enigma this woman was.

"You'll need to call the police, Miss Bridges. I'll put the kettle on and make some sandwiches. I daresay it's going to be a long night. Let's just hope it was a tragic accident."

It wasn't. My scrutiny had discovered the back half of the skull had been bashed in, it was definitely murder.

I decided to circumvent our local constabulary in favour of calling Uncle Albert. Not because our resident policeman was incapable, he wasn't, but because I knew this particular case would need a specialist.

Albert was the current Police Commissioner with Scotland Yard. He was actually Ginny's Godfather, but insisted we all call him uncle. Luckily he was available when I called.

"Ella, what a pleasant surprise. How are you? Settling in well at the cottage and no more ghostly goings on, I hope?" he finished in a whisper.

Albert had been instrumental in helping me solve the case of a murdered young orphan girl not long after I'd moved in. He'd also met Phantom and ruined a perfectly good shirt in the process. I'm not sure he'd fully got over the shock.

"Actually, Uncle Albert, there are more ghostly goings on as you put it, and I'm afraid it's in your professional capacity I'm calling. I've found a body. Well, a skeleton actually, hidden behind one of the panels in the down-stairs dining room."

"Good lord, have you really? What a shock for you. Are you all right?"

"Yes, I'm fine, but wondered if you could help. I'm not sure what to do next."

"Of course I'll help, Ella. That goes without saying. Now if you'll give me all the details, I'll make some notes and get the ball rolling at this end."

I could hear the scratching of Albert's pen while he scribbled extensively, stopping a couple of times to con-firm what I'd said.

"And you think it's murder, do you?"

"Well, the back of the skull is extremely damaged, much more so than if she'd simply fallen down the stairs. It looks deliberate to me, very nasty." I looked around to make sure Mrs. Shaw wasn't hovering about and lowered my voice. "Plus, of course, the ghost of a woman has been in residence since I discovered the room, and judging from the jewellery, the body's definitely hers."

"Ah I see, yes. Well, leave it with me. I'll start things moving here. I'll also see to it word gets to your local chap. Not that we're likely to need him, of course, more a matter of courtesy. I should be with you in a couple of hours at most."

"I'll have the guest room made up for you. Thank you, Uncle Albert," I said and rang off.

Back in the kitchen Mrs. Shaw was buttering bread and slicing luncheon meat as though the entire greater London constabulary would descend at any moment.

"I think that will do actually, Mrs. Shaw. I'm not sure how many will be coming, but Albert Montesford will be staying overnight so will require dinner. Also, could you make up the front guest room for him, please?"

"Certainly, Miss Bridges. Oh, and while I remember, there's a package for you there," she nodded to the dresser, "from Miss Dinworthy. Giles was on his way over when he saw me in the village, so he kindly dropped me off. He also said to expect the gardener at nine in the morning. Oh, and here's your notebook."

"Thank you, Mrs. Shaw." I made a note about the gardener, put the notebook and pen in my pocket next to the matches and went to the dresser.

I opened the package to find a small wicker basket full of items. Dried lemon balm and chamomile in paper packets, recipes for the teas as she'd promised and several packets of vegetable seeds, so I could grow my own once I had my garden up and running, the accompanying note said. *Dear Harriet, how thoughtful.* Plus three large red onions. I scanned the note again, wondering what they were for: stewed onion syrup, soup, or eat them raw. I grimaced. Better stick to the tea. Putting them to one side, I informed Mrs. Shaw I would be in the room behind the pantry if she wanted me, and set off to explore the newly-found staircase. I needed to know where it went.

I took a candle, much quicker than trying to hunt for the torch I wasn't sure I'd brought with me when I'd moved, and gingerly stepped over the remains, being careful not to disturb anything. I began to ascend into the gloom. It was much wider than the staff stairs and would easily accommodate guests with the full skirts of a long-ago era. It was clear by the amount of dust and thick cobwebs, this staircase had not been used for aeons. The walls were panelled in a similar fashion to the main room, with a handrail affixed to one side, but the steps themselves were bare stone and uneven from use. The light from the candle was poor, so I had to take my time, but my feet still kicked up many years' worth of dust, causing me to cough and sneeze.

I shivered as thick cobwebs stuck to my hair, and stifled a scream as I felt something drop on the back of my neck. Slapping wildly at my unseen assailant, I dropped the candle and watched as it bounced down a couple of steps and the flame died. With shaking hands, I took the matchbox from my pocket and striking the head produced a flame. Lowering it in search of the candle, I came face to face with a pair of green eyes. I fell back on the step, heart pounding and gasping with fright. The match flame guttered for a second, then went out.

"Phantom! That was not funny," I hissed, as I shakily produced another flame and managed to relight my errant candle. Phantom sat on the step with a smug look on his face. I turned, ignoring him, and continued my journey upwards.

The tickling of another multi-legged creature crawling up my calf induced a strange dance, as I stomped my feet trying to dislodge it. Which, of course, raised more dust and set me to sneezing again. With eyes streaming, I eventually came to a dogleg and with one hand guiding me around the wall, turned left and continued. Surely it couldn't be much further. Several steps more and I finally reached a small landing and what looked like a solid door. I leant my head against it in relief. I felt as though I'd climbed a mountain.

"Well, this is it," I said to myself. "Let's see where you lead to." I put my shoulder against the door, pushed, and nothing happened. I frowned. Of course there must be a hidden catch of some sort released from the other side, but this side it should be easy to spot. It was, about halfway down the left side. I lifted it and the door swung outward about an inch, letting in a much welcome shaft of light and clean air.

After so many years of disuse, I had expected it to be stiff, but with a gentle push, it swung easily and I found myself in the formal reception room. Turning, I saw the secret panel was in fact the left side of a pair of bookshelves, which encompassed the fireplace. I pushed it shut again and stood back to gaze at the clever concealment. I doubted I would ever have found it from this side. Now I knew what to look for I found the mechanism easily. Once again it was a small piece of ornate carving in the fire surround, which when depressed freed the catch with a barely perceptible click.

Nodding at a job well done, I found myself in a cloud of dust and cobwebs. Dashing to the mirror in the hall, I laughed at the stranger staring back at me. I looked like the Ghost of Christmas Past. *I'd better get cleaned up before Albert arrives. It wouldn't do to give him any more frights.*

I'd donned a pair of dark green twill trousers with a leather belt, and teamed them with a matching sweater and brown and white Oxford saddle shoes. Considering my work for the day, my tweed skirt, stockings and heels were an impractical choice. Plus I secretly felt far more comfortable in this attire than the former. It was quite liberating.

By the time I reached the kitchen, Albert was already there, a delicate cup of tea in one meaty hand and a sandwich in the other. Mrs. Shaw frowned briefly at my choice of clothing, but wisely kept her own counsel.

With Albert were two other gentlemen I didn't know, each with their own victuals.

"Ella, may I introduce the police surgeon Doctor Mortimer Smythe?"

"Miss Bridges," the doctor said in a reedy tone, and with a serious look, shook my proffered hand. Wearing a sombre grey suit he was excessively tall and thin, with a bald pate and a grey toothbrush moustache. He was also extremely pale. He obviously spent many hours working indoors. I noticed in him the tell-tale signs of an habitual pipe smoker and didn't want him to feel awkward.

"Do feel free to smoke your pipe indoors, Doctor Smythe. I don't mind in the slightest."

He raised an eyebrow, shot a glance at Albert, but said nothing.

"And this is Sergeant Baxter."

The sergeant raised his sandwich in embarrassed response, and mumbled through a mouthful, "Miss." In contrast he was of ruddy complexion and had a short stocky build. Mid-brown hair, beginning to grey at the temples, was swept back from a wide forehead, but the crinkling around the bright intelligent eyes spoke of an easy humour.

"Well, gentlemen, I see my housekeeper has been looking after you. Thank you, Mrs. Shaw. Now if you've all finished, I'll take you through."

I unfastened the hidden catch, slid the shelf sideways, and the three gentlemen followed me.

Albert held me back momentarily and said in a low voice, "Well done, Ella, regarding the pipe, and what did you notice about the sergeant?"

I whispered back. "I do believe he had eggs for breakfast."

Albert let out a guffaw, then proceeded to the far end of the room where the panel was still open.

"It's a bit dark in 'ere," Sergeant Baxter said. "Is it only candlelight you've got, Miss?"

"The rest of the house has electricity, but I'm afraid it's all we have in here until I can sort out the wiring."

"Sergeant, if you'll assist the doctor," Albert said.

"Yes, sir. I'll start by bringing in the portables," he said and left.

"Portables?" I asked Albert.

"Lanterns. They're a standard part of the field kit. You never know what you're going to find or where you're going to find it."

Albert looked at the skeleton with a sad shake of his head, peered up the staircase and examined the panel. Then came across to where I was waiting. "Ella, we'll stay out of the way for the moment, let Mortimer do his job. Perhaps you can show me where the staircase emerges?"

I nodded and led him upstairs.

"I thought it best we spoke privately, considering the nature of your, er … unusual ability," Albert said when we'd reached the safety of the reception room.

"Oh, quite," I said. "Wouldn't want to upset the natives."

"It's a remarkable room you've discovered there. Must have been quite a surprise?"

"Absolutely, but terribly exciting too. I'm looking forward to using it."

"I'm not sure Ginny will be too keen. I telephoned and told her I was on my way here and why. She likened it to a medieval banqueting hall, full of Vikings with appalling manners," Albert said with a smirk.

I laughed; that was just like Ginny. My sister-in-law had a penchant for drama.

"And you've no idea whose remains they are?" he asked.

I did have a possible idea, but until I was sure I didn't want to say anything. "Not at the moment, but I'm in the process of doing some research. I'll let you know what I find out."

Albert nodded in acceptance. "Well, the doctor should be able to give an approximate age of the bones which should help. I'll pass on what information he gleans. So show me how this door works. I must say I'm intrigued. I've been looking, but can't spot it."

I rose and went to the fireplace. "Keep your eye on the left bookcase," I said and depressed the catch. The bookcase swung forward about an inch revealing the dark space beyond.

Albert went to study it in more detail. "Remarkable. And what craftsmanship. I'll get Baxter to add some lights down there. It will make the job easier."

He called down and the sergeant responded with a, "Yes, sir."

"Will they be staying overnight too? If so, I'll need to let Mrs. Shaw know."

"No, I've arranged for rooms at the Dog and Gun in the village for tonight. With any luck we'll be able to move the deceased tomorrow. She'll be taken to the morgue and Mortimer will continue the examination there."

A few minutes later, Sergeant Baxter appeared with several lanterns and we left him to it.

CHAPTER NINE

A couple of hours later, Albert and I were seated at the large table downstairs, listening to Doctor Smythe's findings.

"I've confirmed it was a female, although with the presence of the jewellery it was rather a moot point. I've bagged those here for you, Miss Bridges." He slid a buff-coloured envelope across the table to me. I must have looked surprised for he continued, "I believe they will be safer in your keeping until a next of kin is found, assuming there is one. It's always difficult with cases as old as this."

"And what happens if there is no next of kin?"

Albert answered, "Unless they're of particular importance to the nation or the crown, then they're yours to do with as you wish. In essence, you bought them along with the contents of the property."

"Good heavens, I had no idea."

"What else did you discover, Doctor?" asked Albert.

"You're quite right about it being murder. The trauma to the back of the skull is considerable. She was repeatedly hit over the head with a blunt, heavy instrument and in my opinion this was excessive. A vicious attack. Whoever did it was extremely angry."

"Yes, I thought so too," I said. "The first blow would have killed her outright, wouldn't it? Then why continue to lash out unless whoever did it was in a blind rage about something she had done."

"You ought to offer her a job, Albert," Doctor Smythe said in all seriousness.

Albert eyed me with interest as the doctor continued.

"Her neck is also broken, as are her left wrist and ankle, but they happened post-mortem, most likely when she was thrown down the stairs."

"It's definite she went down the stairs then and wasn't shoved behind the panel from this room?" asked Albert.

To his surprise, I answered."Yes, it is. I noticed some scuffs down the panelling when I went up the stairs. There are also some old stains which could be blood, and a couple of the pearls from the broken necklace in the corner of the upper treads." I rattled the contents of the envelope for emphasis.

"Is there any way to tell her age? I don't mean how old the bones are, but what age she was when she died?" I asked.

The doctor's lips were twitching in a half smile as he answered. "Well, I'll have a better idea when I get back to London, but there are no obvious signs of age related deformity. That, together with the fact the bones are fully matured leads me to make an educated guess at somewhere between twenty-five and thirty."

She'd been the same age as me.

"It's purely guesswork, you understand," said the doctor, "and not something I do under normal circumstances. It also depends on a number of external factors, you see, such as diet and living conditions, which I won't know until we can put a more definite age to the bones themselves."

I nodded. "Of course. One other thing, is it possible to know whether she'd given birth?"

"While we've made great strides in this area of science, Miss Bridges, I can't help with that particular question. But there is one other point of note. She was missing the last joint of the little finger on her right hand. It could have been a birth defect or a prior accident, difficult to tell now of course, but it may help identify her. Now if you'll excuse me," he said rising, "there's nothing more we can do today. Baxter and I will get on with the photographs and suchlike in the morning, then we can move her to London."

"I'll see you out, Mortimer," said Albert, heaving his great bulk from the chair.

Doctor Smythe turned to me and held out a hand. "It's been a pleasure, Miss Bridges. I seldom meet a mind as bright as yours."

"Well, you've certainly impressed Mortimer. I've rarely heard him speak so highly of anyone at a first meeting,"

Albert said when he returned. "Now what do you say I take you out for dinner this evening?"

I agreed that was a lovely idea, and after I'd informed Mrs. Shaw, who assured me there was nothing she had prepared that wouldn't be perfectly fine for the next day's lunch, we went to dress.

I woke with a start the next day and dashed out of bed to the phone. The dinner party was the following day and I still hadn't organised a suitable gift. With the police in my house, the gardener due, no suitable boutique in the village in which to purchase something and no time to go to London myself, I called Ginny.

"Of course I'll help, Ella. Since when have I ever refused a shopping trip? I'll pop along to Harrods later and have them deliver something to you today. But do let me wake up first. I know you rise earlier in the country, but it's still the middle of the night here. Goodbye, darling, talk soon," she said with a yawn and put the telephone down.

I laughed and replaced the receiver. Ginny already treated my island home as though it were a different country with its own weather system, and now it would appear, a different time zone as well.

I reached the dining room and found Albert helping himself to breakfast. The various covered dishes on the sideboard contained bacon, eggs both scrambled and fried, sausages and fried bread. Not to mention several rounds of toast with preserves as well as tea and coffee.

"Good morning, Ella."

"Goodness, Mrs. Shaw has been busy this morning. She must have been up before dawn," I said in amazement. I helped myself, then sat across from Albert and poured us both tea.

"What time will Doctor Smythe and Sergeant Baxter arrive, do you think?" I asked Albert.

He removed the napkin from his knee, wiped his mouth and, glancing at his wristwatch, said, "In about half an hour, I should think. Mortimer is an early riser and there's a lot to do before we set off back to London. I'd imagine you'll find the next bit interesting. Are you staying to watch?"

"I'd certainly like to, yes. I'm expecting a young man to interview for a gardener's position, but that shouldn't take too long. I need to see she's taken care of. That probably sounds silly, doesn't it? But I feel responsible for her and I'm wondering if her spirit will move along with her remains."

"Do you think it will?"

"I'm not sure. I haven't solved everything yet. I mean, we don't even know who she is, so perhaps not. But we do know she was murdered, which is something, I suppose. Ultimately, she's here seeking justice."

"In my experience, once we identify her it should make finding the murderer easier. It's all about those with a motive and the means to commit the act," Albert said.

"Yes, you're right. Well, all we can do is wait and see. If she stays, then I know I have more to do."

Albert put his napkin on the table and sat back, his breakfast finished.

"You know, I was reading a piece in The Times the other day about that Conan-Doyle chap."

"The writer? I believe Jerry met him a couple of times before he died. Only briefly, you understand, and more as an admirer, as it was before Jerry really became known. Have you read any of his Holmes books?"

Albert raised an eyebrow. "The violin playing, opium smoking, master of disguise detective and his greenhorn sidekick? No, not a word," he said with a twinkle in his eye.

I smiled. "Not quite true to life then?"

He shook his head. "Not quite, no. But they are written from a refreshing angle with some astute observations. I find them very entertaining. But that's not why I mentioned it. Did you know he was a spiritualist? He's written much about his beliefs and used to lecture on the subject."

"No, I didn't know that." I frowned as I tried to recall a fleeting memory. "Wasn't there something about him and the Cottingley fairies? Jerry and I grew up near there."

"That's right, he was a true believer. He published a book about them, all part and parcel of his belief in the spirit world. His children's nanny had psychic abilities as it turned out. I'll try and dig out the article for you. It's fascinating stuff."

"Thank you, Uncle Albert, I'd be most interested to read it. I'll make a note to see if Harriet can obtain some of his spiritualist books for me." I took my notebook from my pocket and had just finished scribbling when Mrs. Shaw came in to announce the arrival of Albert's colleagues.

"They're busy unloading a lot of equipment in the yard, sir," she informed him, beginning to clear the table.

"I'll come and unlock the pantry door for them," I said.

"There's also a young man loitering at the gate, Miss Bridges, the gardener most likely. I think he's a bit nervous of coming in, what with the police being here and everything."

Heavens, I hoped he wasn't a criminal. No, Harriet wouldn't have suggested him if that were the case. In a very unladylike way, thanks to my trousers, I took the stairs at a canter while Albert made steadier progress behind me. I unlocked the pantry door, then went out to the yard.

Shouting a "Good morning," to the policemen, I walked down the drive to the gate.

There, a tall, thin young man stood shivering in a much patched jacket and worn boots, twisting a flat cap in his hands. His face was pink with both the cool morning air and undoubtedly a good scrub of a flannel by the same person who had lovingly repaired his jacket. His pale blond hair had been flattened to within an inch of its life by what looked suspiciously like lard, and he also seemed to have brought a wheelbarrow with him. I doubted he'd need it though. The old barn had every conceivable tool a gardener required. It was one of the first things I'd checked.

"Hello, I'm Isobella Bridges. Did Harriet, Miss Dinworthy, send you?"

In response, he pulled an envelope from his pocket and handed it to me with a shy smile. It was a note from Harriet.

Isobella dear,

This is Tom Parsons, the young man I mentioned to you. He is a dear sweet boy and an innocent, if you comprehend my meaning. He speaks very little, but understands everything you say. I must mention he has an aversion to being touched. It distresses him greatly, even something as simple as shaking hands. He and his parents live in one of the fishermen's cottages and his mother cleans at the hotel, which is how I came to know him. He has been my gardener for the past year and has worked absolute wonders here. Do visit when you get a chance and I'll show you around. Unfortunately there just isn't the amount of work needed as there once was, more a case of keeping on top of things really. I'd gladly keep him on full time, but I can see he's frustrated and eager for a challenge, something to stretch his mind and his talent. Your walled garden, for example. Let me know how you get on.

With best wishes,
Harriet.

P.S. I hope the tea did its job.

"Thank you, Tom. Harriet speaks very highly of you and the work you've done for her. Come in and wait while I get my coat, then we can take a walk around the gardens and I'll show you what needs doing. I do believe Mrs. Shaw has some breakfast going spare."

CHAPTER TEN

While Tom was devouring the remainder of the breakfast in the kitchen, I wrote a letter to his mother. I wanted to introduce myself as Tom's potential employer and to allay any fears she might have. I suspected they were having difficulty making ends meet, but she would be protective of her son and wouldn't let him work for just anyone, he'd be far too easy to take advantage of. I'd said I would be at her cottage at three that afternoon, but if it wasn't convenient to telephone me. I doubted they had a telephone, but knew there was a call box not far away.

That done, I put it in an envelope for Tom to give to his mother when he returned home and went back to the kitchen.

Tom and I had a leisurely stroll around the gardens for almost an hour. I pointed out the lawns which were in dire need of mowing. Trees and bushes needing pruning, hedges needing cutting and various beds and borders which needed bringing back to life. A lot of it was more akin to an archaeological dig than gardening, but I sensed Tom's excitement as we explored. Finally, we came to the immense barricade of weed and briars I had mentioned to Harriet.

"I realise this is a huge undertaking, Tom, and it will take a considerable amount of time to clear. But Harriet and I believe at the back of this lot somewhere there is a walled garden."

He looked at me in amazement, eyes wide and a huge grin on his cherubic face.

"I know, that was my initial reaction too. I'd dearly love to start it up again, produce vegetables and fruit and whatnot. Do you think you'd be up for that?"

He took off his cap and began to twist it. Finally, looking up, he stammered, "Y-yes, Miss. Please."

I was thrilled, not just because he'd spoken, which I hadn't expected after Harriet's note, but because he'd said please. That simple little word spoke volumes.

"Then I would be very pleased to offer you a position here as head gardener, Tom. Here, I've written to your mother. Could you give it to her when you go home? I'd like to visit and introduce myself this afternoon if it's convenient."

He nodded and taking it, carefully put it in his pocket. Then replacing his cap, he ambled off in the direction of the gate. Halfway there he turned round and waved cheerfully before picking up his wheelbarrow and disappearing.

I smiled and went back indoors to telephone Harriet.

Harriet was tremendously pleased I'd taken Tom on and even happier when I'd said I was going to meet his mother. I also thanked her for the basket of goodies she sent, which she said was no trouble at all.

I rang off, saying I'd see her at The Hall for dinner the next evening, to which she replied with a strange non-committal grunt, and I set off back to the dining room and the police.

Mrs. Shaw caught me in the kitchen to say she'd be leaving at noon sharp to go up to Arundel. "There's a lot to prepare for the dinner tomorrow night and I said I'd help."

I assured her that would be fine.

The ghost of the lady was still hovering around the fireplace when I entered, visible to no one but me, and I also spied Phantom asleep in one of the chairs, one green eye opening to fix me with a stare as I entered, then closing again, disinterested.

Albert was at the table concentrating deeply on paperwork and Doctor Smythe was peering through the lens of a camera, so I wandered over to see what Baxter was doing.

"Why, Sergeant Baxter, what an incredible talent you have." I peered over his shoulder and watched mesmerised as, bent over a drawing pad he drew sections of the skeleton in meticulous detail.

"It's incredible how you make the bones come alive."

He snorted and I giggled, realising what I'd said. I wondered what his reaction would be if he knew the woman's shade was in the room with us.

"You make it look so easy. Did you have training?"

"No, self-taught. Art was hardly a job for a man. Not when I was a lad and probably not now. No money in it unless you're in the business end, buying and selling and so forth. I was expected to follow in my father's footsteps and join the police force, so that's what I did. Mind you, I always carried a sketch book with me, even during the war."

"It must be gratifying to be able to combine both skills now then?"

He nodded over to Albert. "Your uncle's a good man. Recognises the strength of his men and positions them accordingly."

I glanced over at Albert, who was giving an excellent impression of being perfectly oblivious, but I wondered.

Leaving Baxter, I went to watch the doctor.

"Ah, Ella, come to learn? Good, good. You can be my assistant. Now, if you could hold this light and illuminate that area there, a little higher, perfect. Stay still … got it. Now up a couple of steps, that's it. Hold the light lower. I want to get the angle of the head."

We went along in this vein for some time, me holding lights and the doctor taking photographs. Then he asked if I wanted a try with the camera.

"I'd love to, although I'm not sure what's left to photograph."

He remained silent, waiting. I began to walk around the skeleton, talking to myself as I did so. "You've covered the position of the body in relation to her surroundings. The breakages, such as the neck and the traumatised skull and the missing digit. Have you done the scuffs up the panelling?"

He nodded.

"The possible blood stains and the broken pearls on the stairs?"

Again he nodded.

I frowned, what was I missing?

"Ah, the jewellery!" I said triumphantly.

He smiled and shook his head. "I did those quickly yesterday before I removed them. They needed to be photographed insitu."

I shrugged. "I'll admit I'm stumped."

He took the camera from me and handed me a lantern. "Take that and have a closer look. A much closer look," he added enigmatically.

Dutifully, I got down on my hands and knees and proceeded to scrutinise. Then suddenly I saw it and gasped. "You've already taken some close-up photographs of this, I presume?" I said, turning toward him.

"Yes, several."

"Then we should be able to move her. Do you think it's—"

"The murder weapon? I shouldn't be at all surprised."

I left to make drinks and laid out the lunch Mrs. Shaw had organised before she'd left for The Hall. Glancing at the kitchen clock, I noticed I had just under two hours before I needed to set off to see Mrs. Parsons.

Carrying the tray back to the dining table, I saw the doctor and Sergeant Baxter carefully removing the bones and placing them in a large wooden box, lined with rough cloth. It was no wonder I'd missed the crucial clue initially as it was only a fraction that showed. The rest was underneath the body and obscured by the rotted remains of the gown.

Looking up, Doctor Smythe beckoned me over. I stared at what had been revealed.

"Is that a Griffin?" I asked.

"It is indeed. Cast Iron by the looks of it. No wonder it did so much damage. It's a bookend, undoubtedly one of a pair. You haven't seen its partner here by any chance?"

I shook my head. "There's nothing here like that, I'm afraid."

The doctor rose from his crouched position and stretched his back. "Let's have a spot of lunch, then we can take the remainder of the photographs. I need to get back to London shortly."

"Yes, I have an appointment in the village soon too."

Lunch was a rather subdued affair. We ate quickly and mostly in silence, each with our own thoughts. I assisted the doctor with lighting and took some photographs, while Baxter continued with his drawings of the murder weapon and Albert remained at the table, scribbling notes.

"You see here, Ella?"

I looked to where Doctor Smythe was pointing with the end of his pen.

"Blood and … oh dear, that looks like hair. Well, there's no doubt this was used to kill her. How awful. What do you think happened exactly?"

"Taking an educated guess, I would say her assailant lured her to the top of the steps under some guise or other, then as she turned to descend, he hit her from behind with the bookend. I would imagine she fell on the top landing where he continued to attack her in a blind frenzy. Once she was dead, I think he threw the weapon to the bottom then pushed the body down the stairs, which broke her neck in the process. She landed on top of the bookend, which is why it wasn't noticeable immediately."

"Then he simply locked the secret doors, covered his tracks and left her here to rot," I said.

"That's about the sum of it, yes. Ghastly business."

I silently agreed. To think I'd been living here all this time with the skeleton of a murdered woman hidden in the walls. *I must find out who she was.*

The cars were packed in record time and I stood at the kitchen door and waved until they were out of sight. Doctor Smythe had shaken my hand and said what a pleasure it had been to meet me, and extended an invitation to visit and see his work in more detail, should I ever be in London.

Albert had enfolded me in a bear-hug saying he'd see me soon. Of course, neither of us expected it to be as soon as it was.

I cleared away the dishes, locked the hidden doors and went to Change for my appointment with Tom's mother.

CHAPTER ELEVEN

A s I set out to walk to the fisherman's cottages, I was pleasantly surprised to feel a warmer southerly breeze. I had the distinct feeling spring was just around the corner, which lifted my spirits no end. On foot and therefore with no need to take a circuitous route through the village, I halved my journey by taking a shortcut through a less salubrious part of Linhay, past The Kings Head. It was the rougher of two public houses which served the island, and there was always trouble of some sort or other there. The Dog and Gun, where Albert had arranged accommodation for his colleagues, was much nicer and attracted a better clientele altogether. Not least because I believed the quality of beer, while more expensive, was far superior.

As I reached the corner of the pub's tall boundary wall, I glanced up and saw Phantom keeping pace with me, skipping nimbly from stone to stone.

There was a huge commotion and noise coming from beyond the wall with whinnying horses and men shouting. Wafts of manure and spilled beer drifted on the air to be joined by the sweat of the drays as they rested, ready for the return journey. It was obviously the day for the ale to be delivered from the brewery as I could hear the thunderous roar as unloaded barrels were rolled down the chutes to the cellars. The sheer pandemonium beyond meant it was impossible to pick out individual conversations, but as I neared the end of the wall where the cacophony lessened considerably, I found myself inadvertently being privy to a rather heated argument.

"I tell you I don't have it!"

"Then you'd better find it, boy, and quick before I'm forced to break something. Rumour has it you're racking up debts all over. Not surprising, the stuff's not cheap, but my boss gets paid first or else."

I involuntarily shuddered at the sheer menace and hatred in the voice of the older man. This was no idle threat.

"Take your hands off me! Don't you know who I am?"

"I don't care if you're Bonnie Prince Charlie himself. The boss wants his money and it's my job to make sure you pay ... one way or another."

"Yes, well he won't get it if you kill me now, will he? Have you thought of that?"

"Now, now, boy, did I say anything about killing? No, no, no, my instructions are to get it 'by any means necessary short of slitting his throat'. Now, how does two broken legs sound?"

"Don't be so ridiculous, man. You can't just go around breaking a chap's legs. I've told you I will have the money soon. In a week, ten days at the most. Now kindly unhand me and let me go about my business, and you can tell your boss I will only deal with him directly in future. I don't take kindly to threats."

It seemed to me that this young man was either extraordinarily brave, particularly stupid or just plain arrogant. I don't believe he realised how serious his situation was. He was obviously highly educated and his speech and accent marked him as belonging to the upper classes, but I didn't recognise his voice. I just hoped he found a way to extricate himself from the predicament before it was too late.

I continued on with the malevolent laughter of the thuggish man ringing in my ears.

I reached Tom's home a few minutes before the arranged time, but Mrs. Parsons must have been watching out for me as the door opened before I could even raise my hand to knock.

"Good afternoon, Miss Bridges, do come in. It's such a pleasure to finally meet you and thank you for your letter. I'm so happy our Tom has a job with you. Thank you for taking him on. It means so much, what with his father being so ill and his older brothers away doing their own work. Here, let me take your coat. Do go through to the parlour. I've lit a fire so it should be warm for you and the kettle's just set to boiling."

Goodness, when would she pause for breath?

As I had originally surmised, they were in straitened circumstances, partially due to Mr. Parsons being an invalid and of poor health, and Tom's wage would be a much needed addition to the family funds. Mrs. Parsons had gone to a great deal of trouble for me. Over tea, served in what was obviously the best china and a delicious Victoria sponge she'd made herself, I learned Tom had been what was termed 'an accident', coming several years after Patrick, who his parents had thought their third and final son, and when Mrs. Parsons herself was getting on in years. The birth had been a difficult one and it was touch and go whether mother and son would survive the ordeal. As it was, Tom had been starved of oxygen for the first crucial minutes of his life, and as a result was slow and found difficulty in learning, but he had always shown a particular love for nature, his mother had said. This was much apparent in the small square patch of land at the rear of the two-up-two-down fisherman's cottage, where Tom had transformed a once ugly and barren piece of bare earth into a tiny cottage garden of their own.

For the duration of my visit to the Parsons house a small gray scruffy little mongrel, with an endearing face and a happy countenance, made himself at home on my feet.

"That's Digger, Tom's dog," Mrs. Parsons informed me. "Tom rescued him from a trap when he was a pup and they've been inseparable ever since. He'll miss Tom when he's working up at your place."

"Well, Mrs. Parsons, I see no reason why Tom and Digger need be separated at all," I said. "Please, let Tom know I am more than happy for Digger to accompany him to work."

I spent an hour and a half with Mrs. Parsons and the conversation ranged from the walled garden and Tom's duties, to his elder brothers and the scrapes they got into as children. She had raised a fine family on little means and most probably with much sacrifice to herself, and I could see she wouldn't accept handouts or help without doing something of value in return. It was a trait I admired and the more I got to know Mrs. Parsons, the more I liked her.

Finally, I took my leave with promises to call again. I also extended an invitation for her to visit the cottage and have lunch with Tom on occasion.

By the time I left, the air had turned cooler and the sky had darkened considerably. It was as though someone had turned the light-switch off. There was no mistaking the imminence of rain, so I walked to the telephone box on the corner and summoned a taxi to take me home. There was no sign of Phantom although that wasn't unusual, but in fact I wouldn't see him again until I sat down to dinner at The Hall.

CHAPTER TWELVE

'd purchased the dress on a whim the last time I'd been shopping in London with Ginny. It was a deep raspberry satin silk, full length, sleeveless, and to my dismay, backless. I'd balked at the idea initially, but Ginny, along with the owner of the exclusive boutique, had assured me it was the epitome of style and grace. "The perfect combination of risqué and modesty, madam," she'd assured me.

This was the first time I had worn it and standing in front of the mirror in my dressing room, I barely recognised the sleek Grecian Goddess staring back at me. The fabric was cut on the bias, the design hugging my body, creating the ultimate feminine silhouette. I'd never looked nor felt as beautiful. Small groups of beaded flowers adorned the neckline, each one with a tiny pearl in the centre, and at the insistence of Ginny I'd had an evening bag and pair of shoes made to match.

I'd swept back my hair and affixed it with a silver and pearl hair-comb, which showed off the pearl drop earrings my mother had given me and I was just fastening the matching cuff bracelet when the doorbell rang. Mrs. Shaw was already up at The Hall, so I grabbed my black velvet cloak and carefully descended the stairs to answer it.

As expected it was Nathaniel.

He let out a low appreciative whistle. "Ella, you look absolutely stunning," he said as he bent low to kiss my cheek.

"Thank you, Nathaniel." I smiled, blushing a little as my heart pounded.

He looked very dapper in his black tie ensemble, tall and slim; it was the perfect outfit to show off his physique."Shall we go?" he said, extending his arm for me to take.

I took the gift from the hall table and we set off.

Ginny had done awfully well with the gift. It was a beautiful globe lamp on a marble base. A vine with leaves in wrought iron entwined the base and rose above on one side to where two love birds were perched nuzzling together. I was sure Robert and Patty-Mae would appreciate it.

"Are you looking forward to this evening?" Nathaniel asked as he drove down the village high street and took a left at the end, to climb the hill to the bluff.

Was I? I found I wasn't altogether sure. I must have hesitated a little too long for Nathaniel suddenly burst out laughing.

"Yes, they're my sentiments as well."

"Oh, no, I didn't mean I wasn't, that sounds terribly ungrateful. This is my first dinner party since I moved to Linhay and I am determined to enjoy myself."

"Your first? Well, we'll have to make amends for that appalling oversight. So what's the trouble?"

"It just seems rather an odd group of people and I'm not sure how well we'll all get on."

"I confess, apart from us and our hosts, I don't know who else will be there."

"The only other I know of is Harriet, but that would mean an odd number so there must be at least one other, I think there's only going to be six of us."

"Harriet? Heavens, you do surprise me. Well, that might liven things up a bit."

"Whatever do you mean, Nathaniel? I understood Robert and she are old friends. It seems only natural he would ask her to celebrate his engagement, wouldn't he?"

"Of course, you're absolutely right, Ella. Forgive me. I spoke out of turn, water under the bridge and all that. I'm sure we'll have a perfectly pleasant evening." And he refused to say another word on the matter.

I'd never been up to The Hall before and as we passed through the huge wrought-iron gates guarded by giant stone Griffins, and began our slow commute down the long gravel drive I felt as though I'd been transported to an enchanted land.

Torches lined either side of the drive, their flickering flames sheltered by the row of beech running parallel to their rear. Entwined within their branches were hundreds of tiny little lights sparkling like stardust.

"Goodness, Robert's certainly pushing the boat out tonight," said Nathaniel.

"I half expect Pan to trot across the drive playing his flute, followed by half a dozen nymphs."

Nathaniel cast me a sidelong glance. "Uncanny you should say that."

"Why?"

"Look ahead," he said, nodding through the windscreen.

We were just coming to the end of the avenue of trees and in the centre of the circular drive was a huge fountain. Up-lit from the base, it cast the enormous central statuary into relief giving it an eerie realism. It was the God Pan sitting on a tumulus of rocks, flute lifted to his mouth, while sitting at his cloven hoofs bare-breasted nymphs gazed in magically-induced adoration, mesmerised by the sweet piercing music.

"It's a shame the water isn't switched on," Nathaniel said as he opened my door. "It would look spectacular in this evening's setting."

Personally I was glad it was dry. Cascading water would give an illusion of animation and it already looked too real for my liking. It was both sinister and evocative, and knowing the history of The Hall as I did, more than a little ominous.

"Good evening, sir, Miss. Welcome to Arundel Hall." It was Sir Robert's butler Hobbes. He took our coats, handing them to a hovering maid, placed our gifts on a side table commandeered for the purpose, then announced, "Sir Robert and … her Ladyship are in the drawing room if you'll follow me."

"Ladyship, Hobbes?" questioned Nathaniel. "Goodness, have they married already?"

Hobbes cleared his throat and continued walking. "Not yet, sir, no. Those are my orders. Here we are. I'll have your car moved to the garages at the rear of the house." He opened the drawing room doors and standing to one side, announced, "Doctor Brookes and Miss Bridges." Then he removed himself quickly shutting the door behind him. I saw no sign of Patty-Mae, but Robert was there to greet us.

"Ella, lovely to see you, my dear, and how splendid you look."

"Thank you, Robert."

I saw Nathaniel's face momentarily blanch in shock at Robert's transformation. He obviously hadn't seen him since the bizarre metamorphosis. Luckily Robert was oblivious.

"Nathaniel, welcome, good of you to come. Pity about your father, do send him my regards."

While Robert and Nathaniel chatted, I glanced into the long gallery style room and spied Harriet sitting alone by the fire, a large sherry in her hand. Dressed in an austere black gown heavily beaded with jet, she reminded me of a mourning Queen Victoria. Oh, dear.

"Hello Harriet," I greeted her.

"Isobella, at last. Sit, sit do."

I hurriedly sat in the red velvet and gold brocade chair next to her, only recently vacated if the warm seat and squashed cushion was anything to go by.

"What an exquisite gown. You look simply delightful, my dear."

"Thank you, Harriet. I wondered if it might be a little too risqué?"

"Nonsense, it's chic and very stylish. You are the embodiment of English elegance, Isobella, and don't let anyone tell you otherwise. Now what's this I hear about you finding a body in your basement?"

I sighed. "Cedric?"

"Of course Cedric. So is it true?"

"Isobella, what can I get you to drink? A sherry perhaps?" interrupted Robert.

Before I could answer, a discordant voice rang out. "Sherry? Oh, that will never do, Bobby. Sherry is for old folk."

I cringed inwardly.

"Oh, silly me. Harriet, of course I didn't mean you," she continued, which just compounded the insult. "Mix Ella a cocktail, honey, she'll just love it."

Our hostess had returned.

"And Doctor Brookes, what a shame your father couldn't come," she said over her shoulder, tottering across to Harriet and me in her ubiquitous heels, a tight, blood-red gown which looked as though it had been painted on, and twirling a gold slim woven tasselled belt.

"Goodness, are all Americans this rude?" I whispered to Harriet.

"No, my dear, they are not," Harriet answered in a shrewd whisper.

I puzzled at Patty-Mae's impoliteness to Nathaniel, a comparative stranger and her guest, but he just shrugged and gave me a wink.

"Ella, honey, so lovely to see you. And what a cute little dress. We could be sisters." She giggled, kissing my cheeks.

Nathaniel momentarily choked in the background, while Harriet snorted in a most unladylike manner, but Patty-Mae was oblivious.

I noticed under the thick, but expertly applied maquillage, pitted scars and the fine redness of dilated blood vessels. A childhood illness perhaps? It surely couldn't be drink?

"Bobby, where are those cocktails? A lady could die of thirst over here."

"Please, don't go to any trouble for me. A sherry will be perfectly fine," I said, but she disregarded my comment with a wave and an irritated glance at Robert.

"I'm afraid I'm rather hopeless at cocktails, Patty-Mae. Perhaps Hobbes could assist?" Robert said, dejectedly eying the mystifying variety of bottles and assorted paraphernalia on the bar top.

I felt a little sorry for him.

"Oh, never mind, Edgar will see to them when he gets here," she said as she affixed a cigarette to a black and diamante holder, lit it and taking a long drag proceeded to blow out plumes of smoke above her head.

"Edgar?" I inquired, for I didn't recognise the name.

"Rutherford," said Robert. "It was rather a last minute decision to make up the numbers, you know, as your father couldn't make it, Nathaniel."

"Now, Bobby, you know that's not true," Patty-Mae said. "I invited Edgar before we knew about that. How could we not have him here? He introduced us, remember?" She leaned over and patted my knee. "If it hadn't been for Edgar, dear Bobby and me wouldn't have met. The least we can do is have him here to celebrate. We owe him our happiness."

"Well, let's hope he doesn't want to make good the debt," Harriet said sweetly, but the comment went over Patty-Mae's head.

Suddenly the double doors banged opened and a young man strutted in. He was devastatingly handsome, thick blond hair with a side parting swept back from astonishingly blue eyes framed with long lashes. His evening suit was of impeccable quality and the cut showed off his broad shoulders, narrow waist and long legs.

Hobbes hovering in the background announced, "Mr. Rutherford."

"Call this a party?" the newcomer asked, laughing. "Where's the music and the dancing?"

I didn't know Edgar Rutherford, had never seen him before, but his voice was unmistakable. It was the young man I'd heard arguing behind the wall of The Kings Head public house.

Patty-Mae rose giggling. "Now, Edgar, behave yourself. I told you it was a quiet get-together. You can make yourself useful by mixing us some cocktails. Robert doesn't know how and Ella and me are just gasping for a decent drink."

Well, really enough was enough, I thought. "Actually, I would much prefer a sherry, if you wouldn't mind, Robert."

"Of course, my dear. Now that I can do," he said gratefully.

Patty-Mae gave me a brittle smile and shrugged. "Suit yourself, sugar."

"Well done, Isobella," Harriet said quietly.

After brief introductions, Hobbes came and announced dinner was served and we all trooped through to the dining room.

"It's all rather ghastly so far, isn't it?" whispered Nathaniel as he escorted me to dinner. "But I suppose it can't get any worse."

Unfortunately he couldn't have been more wrong.

CHAPTER THIRTEEN

The dining table was beautifully laid out with sparkling glassware, highly polished silver and a wonderfully artistic central silver epergne. Filled to overflowing with white calla lilies and delicate pink carnations, the scent was subtle and evocative of spring. Candelabra at either end cast delicate cosy glows over the linen cloth and subtly highlighted the place names.

As expected, our host and hostess were seated at either end and I found myself sitting next to Patty-Mae on my left, with Nathaniel to my right. Edgar was opposite with Harriet on his right next to Robert.

The hors d'oeuvres arrived and, to my delight, six oysters on the half shell nestled on a bed of crushed ice, was placed before me.

Robert smiled at my obvious pleasure. "Well, we could hardly have a dinner party on Linhay without oysters now, could we?"

"Goodness me, no," I replied. "It would be a terrible dishonour to our little island."

"And why would that be?" drawled Patty-Mae, gesturing to Hobbes to refill her glass.

"Linhay is famous for its oysters," Harriet told her. "They have been fished here since the time of the Romans and are transported to London and further afield by the railway. They were a favourite of Victoria, I believe."

"Fascinating," said Patty-Mae, in a tone which suggested it wasn't.

As the first course was whipped away by an efficient waitress and the Consommé Olga arrived, I tried to engage Edgar in conversation. I'd noticed he was sulking rather after being treated like a cocktail waiter by Patty-Mae.

"Patty-Mae tells us you were the one that introduced her to Robert, Edgar. How did you both meet?"

"Oh, you know how it is in the city. I'm always being invited to aristocratic parties, the most popular nightclubs, and opening nights at the theatre. It was at one of those, I can't remember which one now, where we met," he replied. As we delighted over the food he regaled us with humorous stories and anecdotes.

After several minutes, I found my mind drifting. The food was an utter delight, and I could not help but think what a huge help Mrs. Shaw must have been to Robert's housekeeper.

Over the third course of poached salmon with mousseline sauce and cucumbers, as Edgar continued with more of his tales, I thought, *it's little wonder he has so much debt. Gadding about as he described must leave little time for running his parents' wine business and actually earning his money.*

"The wine trade must be doing better than I thought," said Nathaniel, eerily echoing my thoughts, as Edgar paused for breath.

Edgar glared at him. "And what would a small village doctor know about wine?" he sneered, definitely a little worse for wear as he took another large gulp from his glass.

Nathaniel smiled. "Nothing at all, dear chap, just an observation. So Patty-Mae, you've retired from the silver screen, I believe? Such a shame now that the talkies have taken off. Are you not tempted to go back?"

She shrugged, eying him distastefully. "Of course the studios begged me, just wouldn't take no for an answer. They wined and dined me, sent flowers and gifts and I very nearly gave in, I did. For my fans, you know? How could I let them down? But then I met Bobby and my mind was made up. I am going to be a proper wife to my husband. I thought, what does fame and fortune mean when you have the love of a good man? So that was that," she slurred, and giggled in a way that set my teeth on edge.

Harriet caught my eye. It was inconceivable with a voice like Patty-Mae's she would be considered for a talking film. Everything she had said was pure deception and sadly we all knew it, though no one said a word.

Perhaps this was her way of coping with the inevitable, pretend the decision to leave was hers. Even though I hadn't heard of her myself, it appeared she had been successful. It can't have been easy to suddenly find herself cast aside.

"I'm sure your admirers will miss you terribly, Patty-Mae," I consoled her, "but as you say, you're about to embark on a new life, one in which I'm sure you'll be very happy. I'm sure your fans would understand."

"Here, here," said Robert, raising his glass and unfortunately giving Patty-Mae an excuse to refill hers.

Over the lamb, fillet mignon, and chicken, with a wonderful array of side dishes, Harriet asked about the goings on at the cottage recently.

"Yes, I had heard the police had been. Joe, the landlord at the Dog and Gun mentioned he had a distinguished guest, Scotland Yard's police surgeon no less, and an officer staying," said Robert.

My goodness, word does travel fast on this island.

"Yes, that's right. A few months ago, quite by chance I found a hidden room at the back of the pantry … "

"Oh, my, did you really? How excitin'," gushed Patty-Mae.

"Up until a few days ago I hadn't managed to find the access from the main floor of the house, but knew there must be one. I came across the secret door in a panel near the fireplace. I subsequently discovered this led up a staircase to the formal reception room. However, at the bottom of the staircase when I opened the panel, I discovered a female skeleton."

There was a collective intake of breath. "A murder then," stated Harriet, as sharp as ever.

I nodded.

"But how do you know it was murder?" slurred Edgar. "Couldn't she have fallen down the stairs?"

"If it had been an accident I'm sure someone would have missed her, Rutherford. But I think there must be more to the tale. Is that right, Ella?" Nathaniel asked.

"Yes, it is. On further examination, it was obvious her skull had been bashed repeatedly. She was then pushed down the stairs and left there. It was a heinous crime, but it happened over one hundred years ago." I flashed a quick look at Harriet who, with a barely perceptible raised eyebrow, confirmed she understood what I meant. "I'll know more when the police have finished their examination."

The desserts arrived then: sumptuous chocolate and vanilla éclairs, peaches in chartreuse jelly and a divine French ice cream.

"Do you know who she could be?" asked Robert, tucking into his peaches.

"Not really, no, but Harriet mentioned my cottage used to be the Dower House so there is a connection to The Hall. I wondered if perhaps she used to live here or possibly was a relation of some sort?"

"It's possible, I suppose, but I wouldn't know where to start. That's more Harriet's thing. There were various papers and whatnot when I bought the place. I put them all in the attics, but you're welcome to go through them. What do you think, Harriet?"

"I'd certainly be happy to help and the papers are the best place to begin. Ella, let's get together one day this week and make a plan."

"Yes, all right, Harriet, thank you."

"There were some paintings, of course," Robert continued. "Portraits mostly, large heavy gilt frames, subjects looking austere and quite terrifying in one or two, you know the sort. Had a chap in London value them and they're worth a bob or two, quite old he said. Perhaps your lady is one of those? I hung them in the library if you want to take a look. I thought we'd dispense with tradition anyway and all take coffee there."

"If you'll excuse me, I just need to visit the powder room. Do start without me," said Patty-Mae, rising with a wobble and gingerly making her way from the room.

"Feel free to start without me too, old boy. Need a bit of air." And Edgar too lurched his way out of the door.

Harriet and Nathaniel also made their excuses and left, so Robert and I adjourned to the library alone where I hoped I would be able to shed more light on my ghostly lodger.

The library was breath-taking. "What a splendid room, Robert," I said gazing around. The floor to ceiling panels with their intricately designed bookshelves were the colour of rich dark honey and shone with the patina of age.

The hard wooden floor was softened by large hand-woven Aubusson rugs in deep reds, creams and golds.

Row after row of books, with their gold and richly-coloured leather spines adorned the shelves, interspersed with curious objects from around the world. African masks sat alongside inlaid boxes from Asia. A set of mouth pipes from the Andes snuggled next to an eighteenth century French musical box, inlaid with gold in the Rococo style. When the lid was lifted, a delightful singing bird rose up, its beak opening in time with the notes and a fluttering of wings.

In between each of the bookshelves, highlighted by individual gold picture lights, were the various portraits Robert had mentioned at dinner. I perused each one, interested in the names, some of whom I recognised from Harriet's tale of the curse. Most were men and of the three that were female, none of them matched the spirit of the dead woman. I still had to find her, but I felt sure I was getting close.

"Oh, this is interesting," I said.

"What's that, Ella?" asked Robert, sauntering to my side. "Ah yes, the bookend. Unusual I thought, and I rather liked it. Griffins of course are everywhere here. You probably noticed the guards at the gate? They're also on the coat of arms worked into the fireplace over there, and numerous other places. A shame I couldn't find the other. It would have been nice to have the matching pair."

"Actually, Robert, I recently found its twin at the cottage."

"Did you really? Heavens, what a stroke of luck, would you consider selling it?"

"It's no longer in my possession. The police have it. I'm afraid it was the murder weapon, you see."

"Well, that certainly proves there's a connection between the victim and The Hall, Isobella. The sooner we start on those papers, the better," said Harriet brusquely as she joined us. She was flushed and looked upset.

What on Earth has happened?

"Excuse me, Sir Robert, there is a gentleman here to see you." Hobbes had entered in his usual silent manner.

"Gentleman? What gentleman?"

"He wouldn't say, sir. Just that he wished to see you as a matter of urgency and that it was a private matter."

"I see. Do excuse me, ladies," he said, addressing Harriet and me.

When Robert had left I asked Harriet what was wrong.

"What a despicable woman. She's just accused me of having designs on her fiancé. What preposterous nonsense. Robert and I have been friends all our lives, but she threatened me in no uncertain terms to stay away. How dare she? What on Earth was Robert thinking, getting involved with such an abominable creature? I could quite happily throttle the ignorant, ill-mannered hussy."

"Oh, Harriet, how appalling. Would you like me to have a discreet word with her?"

"Absolutely not. I'm perfectly capable of fighting my own battles, thank you very much. Besides she's taking a walk around the garden. I'm afraid I gave her a piece of my mind and she didn't take kindly to the truth." She paused and took a deep breath. "I do apologise, Isobella. I didn't mean for you to bear the brunt of my wrath, but I'm absolutely livid."

I needed to pay a visit to the powder room myself, but I couldn't possibly leave Harriet in such a state. Luckily Nathaniel returned.

"Can I get you ladies coffee?" he asked, moving to the sideboard.

"Please, Nathaniel," Harriet said, lowering herself into one of the plush fireside sofas.

"Not for me at the moment, thank you. I'll help myself when I come back." I moved towards Nathaniel and whispered, "Could you add a splash of Brandy to Harriet's coffee? I'm afraid she's rather upset." He glanced over at her and raised a questioning eyebrow at me. I shook my head and went in search of the powder room.

CHAPTER FOURTEEN

The Hall was a warren of corridors and rooms which seemed to lead nowhere and within minutes I was hopelessly lost. I should have asked for directions, or better still a map. As I rounded a corner and entered yet another hallway, I heard voices. Robert and another gentleman. Not wanting to intrude, I ducked behind a large jardinière housing an enormous palm, and waited for them to leave.

"It's as you thought, sir. I'm sorry to say, a fraud."

"Dear god, what a fool I've been," Robert said quietly. "And the other matter?"

The other man let out a sigh. "I'm terribly sorry, sir, you were quite right, there is someone else involved. It's all in my report."

"You'd better come into the office, Entwhistle. I have guests and this needs to be kept between us, you understand?"

"Of course, sir. Discretion is my middle…"

A door clicked softly and the final words were lost.

I frowned. *What an Earth was that about?* I peeked between the fronds of the palm to ensure they'd gone…

"Ahem," cleared a throat behind me.

I only just held back a scream and spun round. "Hobbes, you frightened me to death."

"I do apologise, Miss Bridges. Are you looking for something in particular?" Neither his voice nor his face gave away any surprise at seeing me hiding behind a large plant and spying on an empty corridor.

"Actually, I was looking for the powder room and became hopelessly lost."

"It's this way, Miss, if you'd like to follow me." And he turned on his heel and went back the way he'd come. Taking a right, then a left, he pointed to a door.

"There you are, Miss. And the library is just there," he said, pointing to another door just a little further along.

I blushed. If I'd just gone right instead of left, I would have found it immediately. Hobbes must think I'm either dim-witted or up to no good, I thought. I found I didn't like either option, but it was too late now.

"Thank you, Hobbes," I said, mustering as much dignity as I could.

He nodded, then left as silently as he'd arrived.

Back in the Library I found Edgar had returned and was lounging insolently in one of the armchairs, long legs stretched out in front of him, staring morosely into yet another glass, this one containing a deep amber liquid. There was no sign of Robert. He must still be with his visitor, but Nathaniel and Harriet were in quiet conversation by the warm fire. I helped myself to coffee and joined them.

"How are you feeling now, Harriet?" I asked.

"I'll be fine, Isobella. I'm sure the worst of it is over."

"It's all rather horrible, isn't it?" I said in a whisper.

"Well, I certainly won't be attending the wedding," laughed Nathaniel.

"Oh, I rather doubt there'll be a wedding," said Harriet. "Not after tonight."

Before I could ask what made her so sure, she changed the subject.

"Now do tell us about your secret room, Isobella. The staircase went up to the main reception room, you said?"

"Yes, it was behind one of the bookshelves. It's opened by this ingenious little catch on the … Oh, I say." I put my coffee cup down and stood up. "Harriet, do you know if Robert has found any secret rooms here at The Hall?"

"Not to my knowledge. But of course we've lost touch recently. I doubt he'd tell me even if he had. I wouldn't be surprised though. The place is old, so there's bound to be some hidden passages."

"Here's Robert now, Ella. You can ask him yourself," said Nathaniel.

"Apologies everyone; a little problem with the boundary wall on the north east side. Sheep all over the paddocks."

I frowned. I didn't think that was what I'd overheard, and why would escaped sheep, as per Hobbes's announcement, be considered a private matter?

Robert cast a disgusted look at Edgar, then helped himself to coffee. "Anyone need a top up? No? Jolly good."

He brought his coffee over and sat with us. "Has anyone seen Patty-Mae?"

"Garden last time I saw," slurred Edgar in the background. "Told me in no uncertain terms to sod off. Charming, after all I've done. Well, we'll see about that ... " he tapered off quietly.

"I see. Well, I'll get Hobbes to look for her if she hasn't come back soon."

"Isobella has a question for you, Robert," Harriet said, giving him a sad smile.

"What is it, my dear?"

"I was wondering if you'd found any secret passages here?"

"Do you know, I haven't. Of course I've never really looked. It wasn't something that crossed my mind, but in light of your findings, I suppose I should. Why? Do you have an idea?"

I got up and went to the fireplace.

"Your fireplace, although the designs are different, is incredibly similar to mine and I posit the same craftsmen were used for both our houses."

"What exactly are we looking for?" asked Nathaniel, joining me and peering at the carvings.

"A slightly raised piece of moulding in the design. It will be barely noticeable and out of the way, so it's not knocked accidentally or apparent to strangers."

Harriet rooted around in her handbag and came up with her pince-nez, while Robert slipped on his spectacles from their place in his top pocket. The four of us studied the ornate surround, reaching out to touch a likely candidate every now and then.

"I think I've found something," said Nathaniel eventually, moving a large brass coal scuttle and the heavy iron and brass companion set.

I crouched behind him looking at the place he was pointing to at the bottom right. Unlike my fireplaces, which were carved with intricate aspects of nature, this one consisted of decorative scroll-work with a cherub at the base on either side. One had a drum and the other, which Nathaniel was studying, had a harp. It was the last string of the harp he was pointing to.

"Yes, I should think that's it," I agreed.

"What an extraordinary piece of work," Robert said. "I would never have discovered it."

"Press it and see what happens," I said to Nathaniel. "We'll keep an eye on the walls. The panel should click and open slightly."

Nathaniel took a deep breath and depressed the harp's string. There was a soft click, and to the left the bottom half of a bookshelf swung forward a few inches, revealing the void behind.

"Well done, Isobella," Harriet said. "An excellent piece of deduction and what a find."

Robert rang the bell-pull in the corner.

"You rang, sir?" inquired Hobbes a second later, who had as usual appeared from nowhere.

"Hobbes," said Robert, "we've found a secret passageway."

"So it would appear, sir. Will you be requiring light?"

"We will. And perhaps you could rouse that fool while we are gone?" he said, nodding to a hebetudinous Edgar, who seemed to have slept through all the excitement.

"It will be my pleasure, sir," Hobbes said with some relish and left.

I looked back at the open panel just in time to see a black tail disappear into the darkness. Phantom had joined us.

Robert pulled the hidden door open, took a few steps forward and peered into the gloom, "There's a staircase leading down," he informed us.

Harriet approached and using a lace handkerchief, brushed away cob-webs and dust from his shoulder. It was an instinctive intimate gesture, yet one Robert accepted as natural. I sighed. I should have realised. No wonder she'd been so upset.

"It's obviously filthy down there," she said, returning her handkerchief to her handbag. "We're hardly dressed to go exploring the bowels of The Hall."

I looked at my beautiful gown in dismay. I certainly didn't want to ruin it, but I desperately wanted to see where the steps led to.

Hobbes returned at that moment, armed with several torches, a pitcher of iced water and several items of clothing.

"I took the liberty of gathering together some more suitable attire for you all, sir." He placed the torches on the table, handed us all various items of clothing, then, throwing the water in Edgar's face, turned and left with absolute decorum.

Edgar shot up out of his chair, looking around wildly. "What the … ?"

I stared, shocked for an instant, then burst out laughing. I couldn't help myself. It was the funniest thing I had ever seen, and done with such aplomb. My estimation of Hobbes had risen considerably. I turned to the others who were likewise in hysterics. Nathaniel was bent double, gasping and clutching his stomach. Robert had his head thrown back and was guffawing loudly. While dear Harriet was wiping her eyes with her lace handkerchief and transferring dust and cobwebs to her face, which set me to laughing all the more.

"It's just not cricket, you know, Harlow, treating your guests in such an abominable way," sputtered Edgar.

"Oh, stop being such a wet blanket," said Nathaniel.

Which of course sent us into fits again.

"And what are you staring at?" Edgar snarled at Hobbes who had returned.

"I thought you might require a towel, sir."

Edgar snatched the towel, giving Hobbes a filthy look.

"Come, Isobella, we need to change," said Harriet, taking my arm.

As we made our way to the powder room, I heard Robert say, "Come on, buck up, Rutherford, you're like a wet weekend."

Harriet and I shared a look and stifled giggles.

Ensconced in the powder room, Harriet said, "Good heavens, where on Earth did Hobbes dredge these up from?" She was holding up a pair of sludge brown dungarees and a bottle green jumper.

Mine were identical, although the jumper was an iron grey. He'd also thoughtfully provided head-scarves and wellington boots. As we changed, I asked Harriet about Hobbes.

"Not the sort of behaviour I'd expect from a butler, although it was hilarious and done with such panache," I said.

"Hobbes is more than a mere servant, Isobella. He was Robert's batman in the war and when Robert was decommissioned Hobbes came with him. As for Rutherford, Hobbes was quite right. That boy is a spoiled brat who doesn't know the meaning of hard work. He's had everything handed to him on a plate since birth and it's done him no favours. When you've lived through such atrocities as Robert and Hobbes, when you've seen friends killed and wounded and driven mad with grief and fear, it's no wonder he has little time for such shallow, selfish people. He got what he deserved in my opinion. Now, how on Earth am I going to squeeze into these?"

After a lot of pushing and shoving and tightening of Harriet's corsets, we were eventually dressed and joined the men in the library.

"What ho! It's the land girls," exclaimed Robert. "That takes me back a bit."

"It's been years since I wore something like this," said Harriet. "I must say I remember it being far more comfortable then, at least I could breathe. I feel like a goose trussed up for Christmas dinner."

"Well, I for one think you look very fetching, Hettie," Robert said, a little flustered.

I glanced at Harriet who tutted, "Nonsense, Robert." Although I could tell she was flattered.

"Are you coming with us, Rutherford?" asked Nathaniel.

"Of course, but I refuse to dress like a farmer," he said, eying the men's rough spun trousers and shirts with immense distaste. Removing his jacket and tie, he rolled up his sleeves. "Right, let's see what treasure's been hiding down there. Finder's keeper's, eh Harlow?" he said with a laugh.

CHAPTER FIFTEEN

The steps were wider and much longer than the ones I'd navigated at the cottage, but just as sepulchral and I was very grateful for the torches. Robert went first, followed by Harriet. I was behind her with Nathaniel to my back and a disgruntled Edgar bringing up the rear.

Years' worth of dust and cobwebs lined this space too and I rather wished I'd had the foresight to tie the scarf around my mouth rather than my hair, as breathing without choking was proving a challenge.

Twenty or so steps down, we reached a dogleg to the right and continued to descend, then about the same distance further on we turned right again.

"I think we just went around the chimney," said Nathaniel.

"Not much further now," said Robert, "I think I can see the bottom."

A few minutes later we were stood side by side in a cavernous space, where even our powerful lights couldn't penetrate the darkness much more than a few feet in front of us. It was damp and musty smelling, but at least the floor was dry. By unspoken agreement we began to move forward as one, shining our torches into obscure corners and lighting up partial objects not seen for decades. The space as far as I could see was packed to the gills with disused furniture and goodness knows what else, all stored in such a way as to leave walkways amongst the towering objects. It was like a labyrinth.

"Do you think these cellars run the whole width of the Hall?" asked Nathaniel.

"I wouldn't be surprised," said Harriet. "We're at a subterranean level below the kitchens and staff quarters, I think. I doubt it's a continuous space, more a series of inter-joining rooms with the load-bearing walls probably mirroring those upstairs. But it will cover a huge area."

"There's access to some of the cellars from the kitchen. But I suspect these have been walled off somewhere with this stairway as the only access now. I certainly never knew about it," said Robert.

"We need to be careful," I said. "It will be easy to get lost down here."

"Ella's right. It's dangerous too. Half this stuff looks as though it could topple at any moment. I think we should go back upstairs," said Robert.

"Good god, this stuff's priceless. You've really hit the jackpot here, Robert."

I wasn't the only one who'd noticed how solicitous Edgar had suddenly become.

"I bet it's wine and Edgar wants to make a deal," whispered Nathaniel in my ear.

He was right. A tall set of shelves against the left wall was stacked with wine bottles, each with a layer of grime so thick it obscured the label. Edgar had already taken one down and was carefully removing the dust.

He held it reverently as though it were a child. "Chateau Lafitte Rothschild, 1787. The rarest of the rare," he breathed in awe.

Nathaniel whistled. "I'm no oenophile, but wasn't that Jefferson's tipple?"

Edgar looked at him with interest, a small smile crossing his lips. "Not just a simple doctor then. Yes, you're quite right. Jefferson spent a lot of time in France during that time. Robert, this is a superlative find. You simply can't leave them languishing down here forgotten, they need to be out in the world. I can deal with all of that for you, of course. Find the best buyers and organise the auction and so forth. There'll be world interest once the discovery is made known."

"Superlative or not, I haven't got time to deal with all of this now. Just put it back where you found it for the moment, we'll talk about it another time."

"Look Robert, really..."

"Edgar", Harriet interrupted with a warning, "there must be at least two hundred bottles here, all quite possibly of superior vintage, if the first is anything to go by. They need to be handled properly, catalogued and suchlike. I'm sure I don't need to tell you that. These things take time, as you know, which Robert has told you he doesn't have at the moment. He's not dismissing your assistance, just delaying it. Might I suggest you practice a bit of patience for once?"

"Yes, all right, but I want first dibs on them, agreed?"

I didn't wait to see what Robert's response was, for I had spied Phantom disappearing behind a stack of chairs. Following carefully to the right and then to the left I found him sitting in front of a huge object shrouded in velvet dust cloths. Lifting a corner I shone my torch and discovered a large swept frame, somewhat dusty, but still giving off that lustre which only genuine gilt can do.

Resting my torch on a large dresser angled to give me some light, I carefully removed the cloth and found a stack of paintings leaning against a wardrobe. There were six in total, the largest a head taller than I was and heavy. I didn't want to risk moving them by myself so went back for Harriet and Nathaniel.

"I tell you something, Isobella, I didn't expect this Aladdin's cave when we ventured down here. It's an historian's dream. I only hope I live long enough to go through it all. Now what have you found?"

"Portraits by the look of it, old ones too, I would imagine. Looking for the owner of your skeleton, Ella?" Nathaniel said.

"Yes. I feel sure there must be something here to mark her life, connected as she was to The Hall. Could you help me move them?"

"Of course. You take that end. Now carefully, let's stack them one at a time over here."

As Nathaniel and I moved the paintings, Harriet called out the names from the brass plaques attached to the frames. After the fourth one I was beginning to doubt my confidence, and then we unveiled the fifth.

"That's her," I said. "Oh, Harriet, we've found her."

"How do you know?" asked Nathaniel, who hadn't been privy to either the tale of the curse or the discovery of the bones.

"I recognise the jewellery. She was murdered wearing exactly the same items. Harriet, is it who I think it is . . . ?"

Harriet wiped the plaque, then peered through her pince-nez. "Who do you think it is, Isobella?"

"Mary-Ann, the Eleventh Duke's missing wife."

"Then, yes, you're quite correct. It looks as though she was murdered after all."

I was thrilled I had solved the mystery of my ghostly guest, although I couldn't help also wondering what had happened to her lover. Mary-Ann had been restless for nearly one hundred and thirty years, waiting for someone to discover she'd been murdered, and what remained of her body. Now I could arrange a suitable interment and allow her to rest in peace.

However, my elation was short-lived and our own peace shattered with the panicked arrival of Hobbes.

"That's most unlike Hobbes, I wonder what's happened," said Harriet. "Come on."

We hurried back to the main steps to find Hobbes, in an extreme state of agitation.

Hobbes was just shaking his head repeating, "I'm sorry, sir. I'm so sorry, sir."

Robert looked at Harriet in despair. "I can't get a word out of him, Hettie. Damned unusual."

I approached Hobbes and laid my hand on his shoulder. "Can you show us what's troubling you, Hobbes?" I asked gently.

He looked at me with blank eyes. I didn't think he had understood me at first, but then he focused, gave a sharp nod and headed back up the steps. The rest of us followed in puzzled silence.

We all piled back into the library, the light coming as a bit of a shock after being in the gloom for so long, but Hobbes didn't stop. We went after him as he marched from the library, down the hall and back into the foyer. Across the foyer he opened the large front door and went down the steps to the drive. On the lawns I saw a figure, and was about to speak when I realised who it was.

"Oh, no," I whispered.

Nathaniel glanced at me, a concerned look on his face. "Hobbes is in shock, I recognise the symptoms. Whatever has happened has shaken him to his core."

I nodded. I wasn't surprised. I now knew what had happened.

We continued around to the side of the house where

a large evergreen Azalea bush was showing signs of bud. Here Hobbes stopped.

"It was the dogs that found her, sir," he said shakily.

I moved forward and saw the body of Patty-Mae squashed under the bush at an unnatural angle. Her blank eyes staring, no longer seeing anything, and around her throat her gold tasselled belt. She'd been strangled. Glancing back across the lawn I saw her ethereal figure watching me.

Nathaniel checked for a pulse. Rising, he shook his head. "I'm sorry. I'm afraid she's dead."

"Oh, dear god," said Robert, staggering forward.

I grabbed his arm to stop him. I'd learned a lot over the last couple of days. "No, Robert, you mustn't. The police will need to look for evidence, I'm so sorry." I gently pulled him back and spoke to Hobbes. "Hobbes, go and get Mrs. Shaw, please. You'll find her in the kitchen."

He looked at me blankly.

"Hobbes," I shouted. "Go and get Mrs. Shaw. Now, please."

"Yes, Miss Bridges."

I looked at Harriet. She was as still and pale as a marble statue.

"Harriet?"

She looked up.

"Can you take Robert inside and get him some hot sweet tea?" I asked her. "Ask Mrs. Butterworth to make a pot. I think we'll all need it"

She nodded and moved toward Robert.

"Nathaniel, where's Edgar?" I asked.

"By the fountain."

We both looked over to see Edgar being violently sick.

"Can you take him inside and make sure everyone is settled and warm and has something for the shock?"

"Of course. I have my bag in the car in case they need something a little stronger than tea. But I won't use it until absolutely necessary. I daresay we'll all need our wits about us when the police arrive. Shall I call them?"

I shook my head. "No, I'd rather do it if you don't mind. I'll speak to Albert Montesford."

As Nathaniel half carried, half dragged Edgar back to the house, Mrs. Shaw came rushing over.

"Dear God, is it true? Hobbes said Miss Ludere's been killed?"

"Yes, I'm afraid it is. Mrs. Shaw, I need you to stay here and make sure nobody touches anything. The police will need to investigate the area. I'm sorry. I know it's not a pleasant task, but I'm afraid there's no one else I can ask."

"I understand. Of course I'll stay. You get on with calling the police. The sooner they arrive the better, I think," she said, glancing at the body and crossing herself.

I made my way back to the house in a state of shock. Patty-Mae was difficult, uncouth and outrageous, and she'd been terribly rude to most of us during the evening, but no one deserved to die in this awful way. I stopped halfway up the steps and leaned against the balustrade, my heart pounding enough to burst out of my chest as a horrifying thought struck. One of the people I had dined with this evening was a murderer.

CHAPTER SIXTEEN

Albert had been suffering through a bureaucratic dinner when I'd called and his relief at my interruption was palpable.

"Ella, thank goodness. I believe you've just thwarted some dastardly deeds over desserts," he chuckled. "What a tiresome lot they are. Now what can I do for you?"

I explained what had happened and after a short silence he apologised for his flippancy and said, "I'll depart now. I'll arrange for the local bobby to be with you shortly, and whatever you do, don't let anyone leave."

I assured him I wouldn't.

"And make sure the gates are locked at all times. Once the press gets wind of what's happened, and they will, believe me, they'll be camped outside."

∙∙‹‹◈››∙∙

Just over an hour later, Albert and I were ensconced in Robert's office.

"Let's start at the beginning, shall we?" Albert said. "It was some sort of fancy dress do, was it?"

"Sorry?"

He waved a hand at my clothing. "Not the normal sort of thing you'd wear to a dinner party is it, Ella?"

"Oh, this? Hardly," I said and explained how we'd found and explored the cellars. "I found out who the bones belonged to, Albert. Her name was Mary-Ann and she was the young wife of the Eleventh Duke of Arundel. According to the curse she disappeared some time in 1807."

"Well, that's one mystery solved at least. Mortimer's outside at the scene with Baxter. Not much they can do tonight of course, too dark. But you can let him know, he'll certainly be interested. Now what's this about a curse?"

So I went through everything Harriet had told me about The Hall's history, while Albert made notes in his ubiquitous black book.

"And who else, among the people here I mean, knew about this curse?"

"I really couldn't say. Harriet and myself of course. I can't remember if we discussed it at dinner, but I don't think so. Of course those who've lived here a while most probably do know the story. It's part of the fabric of the island. Why? Do you think it's important?"

"Everything is important at the beginning of an inquiry, Ella. Now I'd like to sit down and get your opinion on certain matters, but before I do, I need to address the guests and the staff. I've asked them all to gather in the library. Shall we go through?"

"You realise of course, Ella, no one is going to be able to leave The Hall until the perpetrator is caught?" Albert said as we made our way back to the others. "I've already asked the housekeeper to make up the necessary beds."

"Oh dear, no, I didn't. It's fine for Robert, he lives here. Harriet and I will also be fine, although we'll need changes of clothes, but Nathaniel is a doctor and the only one on the island. What if there's an emergency?"

"He'll have to arrange for a locum to take over in his absence. I'm sure his father can arrange that."

"What about Edgar? He has a business in the city."

"From what I've heard about that boy I doubt he'll be missed."

"Here we are," I said, opening the library doors. Albert strode in while I hovered in the background taking in the scene.

Harriet was sitting on the sofa staring blankly into the fire. I noticed she'd removed her headscarf and was absentmindedly twisting it in her lap. Robert sat opposite, an untouched snifter of whiskey in a cut crystal glass balanced precariously on one knee. He too was lost in the flames. Edgar was back in his chair, working his way through a bottle of brandy. He looked wretched with his tear streaked face, unruly hair, and splashes across the front of his shirt where he'd vomited. Nathaniel was leaning against a bookshelf, hands in his pockets. He was the only one of the four who moved when we entered.

The staff: Hobbes, Mrs. Shaw, Mrs. Butterworth and the serving girl, whose name I didn't know, were huddled together in the corner next to the door. Mrs. Shaw looked her usual stoical self, and Hobbes, although still pale, had come round. The housekeeper was silently dabbing her eyes and sniffing, with her arm around the girl's shoulders making comforting noises as the youngster sobbed into her apron.

"Thank you all for waiting patiently. I realise the hour is late and you'll be wanting to retire," began Albert.

I glanced at the grandfather clock in the corner. It showed three in the morning. No wonder I felt so exhausted.

"However," Albert continued, "until the murderer of Miss Ludere is caught, you will all have to remain here."

I had expected a clamouring of objection at this announcement, but the only one who moved was Nathaniel. The housekeeper had obviously imparted the news prior to our arrival.

"Commissioner, I certainly appreciate the gravity of the situation, but I'm a doctor and as such need to be available for my patients. I will of course … "

Albert stopped him with a raised hand. "I'm sorry for the inconvenience, Doctor Brookes, but this isn't a request. I suggest you telephone your father in the morning and ask him to arrange a locum in your absence. Now if you'll all see Mrs. Butterworth about your sleeping arrangements, we'll convene again in the morning."

I awoke the next morning to a light tap at the door and Mrs. Shaw entered, carrying a breakfast tray. I looked at the room in confusion wondering where I was. Then it all came flooding back.

"What time is it, Mrs. Shaw?" I asked, stifling a yawn.

"Ten-fifteen."

I groaned. "Half the morning gone already. Is there anyone else up and about?"

"Only the police and the staff. Sir Albert felt it was best everyone had breakfast served in their rooms. I expect he wants to keep people from talking and getting their stories straight."

"Possibly."

"I was allowed back to the cottage this morning. A constable drove me to pick up the things you need and I also telephoned Giles and picked up things for Miss Dinworthy. Her housekeeper had everything ready for me."

"Have you seen Harriet this morning?" I asked.

"No, but Mrs. Butterworth's niece is assisting her. She served you last night, her name's Alice."

I nodded while refreshing my tea.

"Well, if there's nothing else, I'll go down and help in the kitchen. Sir Albert said he'd like to see you as soon as you're ready."

"Thank you, Mrs. Shaw, please tell him I won't be long. Oh, and by the way, the meal was excellent last night. You must have worked very hard. Thank you for helping out. I'm sure Mrs. Butterworth appreciated your help and experience."

She gave a curt nod. "It's a pity it all ended in such tragedy."

I found Albert had set up a sort of command centre in a small drawing room to the south of the house, overlooking the terraces and lawns.

"You've moved from the office," I said.

He nodded, pouring me a coffee from a large silver urn. "I have. Sir Robert said he would prefer it. A lot of private papers and whatnot in the office apparently, although he'll soon find out there's no such thing as privacy in a murder investigation. How did you sleep, Ella?"

"Actually very well considering. I feel quite guilty about it."

"Emotions, Ella. No room for emotions if you want to be a detective."

"Who said I wanted to be a detective?"

He pinned me with a stare.

"Mortimer's right, you know, you have a brain and a knack for this type of work. You shouldn't let it go to waste. Now tell me about the dinner, how did the guests seem? Did they get on or was there some tension?"

"To be honest, it was all quite frightful from the start."

I went on to explain how Nathaniel and I had arrived and been escorted through to the drawing room by Hobbes.

"Patty-Mae wasn't there, but Robert greeted us effusively, and seemed genuinely pleased to see us. I noticed Harriet sitting alone by the fire and left Nathaniel and Robert talking while I went over. She was very relieved to see me, Albert, and urged me to sit down quickly. I did notice the cushion was squashed and the seat was warm, not from the fire, but as though someone had been sitting there a moment earlier. I got the feeling she didn't want whoever it was to come back."

"Go on," said Albert.

"I thought at the time how unusual Harriet's choice of clothing was. It was very austere, black and unforgiving. More suitable for a funeral than an engagement party. I think it was deliberate, a statement of some kind."

"What sort of statement?"

I sighed and went to the window. I felt quite sick. It was easy for Albert to say set aside your emotions, but Harriet was my friend and I was gossiping about her. It wasn't just light-hearted nonsense either, no, this was information that could get her into serious trouble. *But could dear Harriet be a cold-hearted killer?* I found I couldn't reconcile that possibility with what I knew of her. Surely it wasn't possible? But then I remembered her words the night before and a cold shiver ran down my spine and my stomach roiled with fear. What was I to do?

Albert had been patient while I wrestled with my internal conscience, but now he spoke.

"Ella, I know this is difficult for you. These are people you know, consider friends even. But the fact of the matter is Miss Ludere has been murdered and one of these people here is responsible. We owe it to her to see her killer caught and punished."

I turned and slumped into the window seat, my back against the cold pane. At that moment Phantom appeared and jumped into my lap, nudging my hand with his head. He was solid for a change. I scooped him up and buried my face in his fur. It was just what I needed and I think he knew.

"Harriet was far from happy about the engagement," I continued, stroking Phantom as I spoke. "And I think her choice of clothing reflected that. When Robert dropped me off at the library that day, Patty-Mae was with us. Harriet barely recognised Robert…"

"Why was that? Had she not seen him for some time?"

"I'm not sure when she saw him last. She intimated they had drifted apart recently, possibly because Patty-Mae was now on the scene, but he's changed considerably. His clothes are vastly different for one thing. Gone are his tweeds. Now he's wearing pastel sweaters and jackets, white linen trousers and gaily spotted cravats. He's coloured his hair as well."

"Mmmm, trying to keep up with a much younger fiancée, do you think?"

I shook my head. "Actually, I don't think Robert had much say in the matter. He looked uncomfortable when I met him in the village and positively embarrassed when he saw Harriet. I think it was all Patty-Mae's doing personally."

"And how did Harriet react?"

"When they left, I noticed her eyes filled with tears," I said sadly. "I heard her whisper 'silly old fool' and wondered at the time if she meant herself or Robert. Could have been both, I suppose. Harriet and Robert have been friends all their lives."

"And how was she with Miss Ludere?"

"Actually we hardly got a word in edgeways. I think we were both a little shell-shocked. Patty-Mae is…" I gulped, "was, a force of nature. Loud and over the top and used to getting her own way. She quite simply ploughed over the people she met. However, I think she was a shrewd operator and recognised something in Harriet, because she emphasised the word 'old' when she said it was lovely meeting Robert's old friends. She was speaking to Harriet at the time. Then of course she threatened her last night."

Albert looked up sharply. "Threatened?"

"Albert, before I tell you what was said, I want you to know I don't think Harriet killed Patty-Mae. I can't see her as a murderer, she's my friend, and while she can be a bit brusque at times and doesn't suffer fools gladly, she is at heart very kind and considerate."

"Duly noted, Ella. So if you don't think it was Harriet, who do you think it was?"

"I don't know," I said quietly. "I can't believe anyone here did it."

"Well, somebody did and in my experience in cases like this it usually boils down to one of two reasons, love or money. Or both."

"A crime of passion, do you mean?"

"Possibly. Now what of this threat?"

"Harriet told me Patty-Mae threatened her in the powder room after dinner last night. She told her in no uncertain terms to 'lay off her fiancé and stay out of the way or else'."

"And how did Harriet react?"

"She was livid, as you can imagine, but also extremely upset and shaken. It distressed her no end." I took a deep breath. "Harriet's words to me were, 'I could quite happily throttle the ignorant, ill-mannered hussy'."

Albert leant back in his chair and took in the view behind me, brow furrowed as he thought.

"Oh, dear, she's in terrible trouble, isn't she?" I said.

"No more than anybody else at this stage, Ella. Now I think you need a break. Take a walk round the grounds and get some fresh air. It will clear your head. I saw the glistening of water down there." He nodded outside. "Could be a lake. Go and feed the ducks and we'll reconvene here in an hour. I realise while we're all under the same roof, it will be difficult to avoid one another, but if you do happen to speak to anyone, please do not discuss the case or what you and I have talked about today."

"No, of course I won't. I'll see you later," I said, and left to find my coat with Phantom on my heels.

CHAPTER SEVENTEEN

lbert was right. Down the terrace steps through the formal knot garden, down the large sweep of verdant lawn and through a small copse, sat a lake. It was man-made and while not large, I could probably walk around it in less than an hour. It was beautifully proportioned and well established. In the centre sat an island with a weeping willow just beginning to bud, and beneath it a dozen ducks waddled. So comical on land, but once they entered the water with a flutter of wings and a little splash, they glided elegantly and colourfully as the sun glinted off their plumage.

I sauntered along the lakeside path breathing in the fresh air and letting my mind go blank. I stopped to watch as a pair of mallards squabbled in the tall reeds, and looked up to see a raptor of indeterminate breed circling overhead, eyes keenly watching for signs of prey scurrying in the undergrowth.

Dotted here and there were clumps of crocus leaves, their delicate flowers waiting for the warmer weather before pushing up and opening in a riot of colour. A few yards ahead, I spied a bench set back slightly from the water's edge and decided to sit awhile.

I had to agree with Albert. There was no room for emotions in a murder case. I was appalled that one of us could be capable of killing another, but the evidence was there in the form of Patty-Mae's strangled and lifeless body. What was the reason though? Who had a motive?

I hated to admit it, but Harriet was the strongest contender. She'd argued with Patty-Mae, been insulted and threatened by her, and had admitted she'd like to throttle her.

Robert. Would there be any reason for him to want to kill the woman he was going to marry? I couldn't see it. There had been a little tension between them last night, but mostly due to Patty-Mae being a little impatient with him. He had been quite gracious throughout, but she had made him look silly and slow, and old. Of course she'd been instrumental in making him dress like a dandy, but surely he wouldn't have agreed to that nonsense if he hadn't wanted to please her? Then again she had been rude to his guests, which would have chafed against his old world gentlemanly disposition, and she was drinking heavily, which I knew he would disapprove of. But were those reasons enough to kill her?

Edgar Rutherford, as far as I was concerned, was an unknown quantity. I hadn't met him until last night, but he was friends with Patty-Mae and had introduced her to Robert. Had something happened last night to turn him from friend to killer? Patty-Mae had treated him rather shabbily, more as a servant than a friend, and he did mention they had had a bit of a tiff in the garden, which he seemed very upset and angry about. I also knew he was in financial trouble. Had the argument escalated and ended in tragedy?

Then there was Nathaniel. When I'd asked him if he knew Patty-Mae he'd said no, but when we'd arrived last night and she'd seen him, she had been very rude. Would you treat a stranger that way? No, they must have known each other somehow, in which case he had lied to me. And if he'd lied, then there must be more to the relationship than I knew. Enough to kill her? Possibly. Albert and I needed to know more.

I found myself feeling depressed at the thought that Nathaniel had lied to me. *Emotions, Ella!* I admonished myself silently. I was also a little angry. Once again I had taken a person at face value, not looking beneath the surface veneer to what lay below. I'd done that with my husband and look where that had got me.

Deep in thought, I nearly shot out of my skin when two black Labradors appeared out of nowhere, and in a flurry of excited yips and wagging tails tried to get on my knee.

"Goodness, what a rambunctious pair you are," I exclaimed, as I tried in vain to stop them licking my face.

"Colt. Bess. To me. Heel!" shouted a voice behind me.

The dogs clambered down and, ignoring the command completely, ran up the path a little way and promptly launched themselves into the lake.

"I do apologise, Miss," said a breathless Hobbes, coming to stand beside me. "I didn't realise anyone was here. As you can see I've got them under perfect control."

I laughed at Hobbes' unexpected show of humour.

"Don't worry, Hobbes, no harm done. I take it walking duties don't normally fall to you?"

He gave a heavy sigh. "No Miss, they don't."

We watched the dogs in silence for a while. Black shiny heads just visible above the water, they were as sleek as otters and having the time of their lives.

"Well, Miss, I'd better get on. Luncheon will be served shortly in the breakfast room."

I watched him walk down the path, hunched over as though the weight of the world were on his shoulders, and mentally added him to the list of suspects.

I thought lunch would be a very subdued affair, a world away from the dinner we had enjoyed together the previous evening, even though it had been somewhat strained. I was wrong.

Of Edgar and Robert there was no sign, but Harriet was sitting at the table picking at her food, her face drawn and tight.

Nathaniel was at the buffet, helping himself to ham and eggs, so I joined him. Surprisingly, even after all that had happened I was feeling hungry.

"Ella, thank god. I was beginning to worry about you. How are you feeling?"

"Much the same as everyone else I expect, Nathaniel, shocked and upset. It all seems quite unreal."

"Yes, it's a dreadful business. Quite dreadful. Here let me," he said, taking my plate to the table.

"Harriet, can I get you some tea?" I asked, noticing she had nothing to drink.

"Please, dear."

As I gave Harriet her tea and sat opposite next to Nathaniel, she reached across and gripped my hand.

"Isobella, please believe me when I say I had nothing to do with this heinous crime. What I said to you last night was in the heat of the moment. It was a stupid thing to say. I was angry and upset, but I wouldn't have even wished ill on Miss Ludere, let alone killed her."

"Oh, Harriet," I said, squeezing her hand in comfort. "I know it was all said in anger and not like you at all. We'll find out who did it. I promise."

She nodded and gave me a tentative smile, then drawing back her hand began to eat. She must have been awake all night worrying and waiting to speak with me. The three of us ate in silence for a while, each with our own thoughts.

"Are you working with the police then?" asked Nathaniel a few minutes later. "I thought we were all suspects?"

"It's rather a long story, Nathaniel. I've helped the Commissioner with two previous cases, both now solved, and he seems to think I'm in an ideal position to help with this one. I suppose he's right. I was here after all."

"So we've got a spy in the camp, have we?" Edgar said as he stormed in and began to heap his plate with food. "Just what we need. You running back and telling tales of our every thought to the police."

"Oh, for god's sake lay off, Rutherford, you're being ridiculous," said Nathaniel. "Not to mention rude. Although come to think of it, you seem incapable of acting any other way."

Edgar let out a vicious laugh. "Got the hots for our little snoop, have you, Doctor? Well, you're welcome to her."

"Now see here, you impudent…" Nathaniel began, rising somewhat aggressively.

"Stop it, both of you," I shouted, standing so abruptly my chair fell with a crash. "Have you any idea how foolish you both look? Do you really think this is the time or the place? Mr. Rutherford, I don't give a hoot what you either think of me or call me, the fact of the matter is there was a brutal murder here last night, and like it or not someone in this house is responsible. If being a spy is what it takes to catch the killer, then that's exactly what I'll be. Now if you'll excuse me, I have things to do." And with that I marched out of the room and bumped straight into Albert.

"Interesting tactics, Ella," he said with a wry smile.

"Oh, dear, that was stupid, wasn't it?"

"Not at all, keeps them on their toes. Now do you have time to continue our discussion?"

"Of course."

"Tell me what you need to know, Albert," I said, sitting myself in the window seat of the drawing room and taking out my notebook, which Mrs. Shaw had thoughtfully brought with my clothes. I noticed the crossword puzzle from Aunt Margaret tucked in the back. Well, I hardly had time to do that now. I had a bigger puzzle to solve.

"The murderer needed to have both the motive and the opportunity to do what he did," Albert began. "We need to establish those who had alibis at the time of the murder. I've already questioned the staff and all of them, apart from the butler Hobbes, are accounted for. Of those that are left, we need to know what their motive for killing Miss Ludere would be. When was the last time you saw her?"

"When we'd all finished dinner. She left first to go to the powder room and I never saw her again. Edgar followed within minutes saying he needed air, which I think he probably did as he'd drunk an awful lot. Nathaniel and Harriet also excused themselves, which left Robert and me. We both went to the library and were there for a short while together before Harriet returned. Robert was then called away by Hobbes as he had a visitor, and he'd just left when Nathaniel returned, which gave me a chance to pay a visit to the powder room myself without leaving Harriet alone. She was upset due to the confrontation with Patty-Mae I told you about earlier. Unfortunately, I got hopelessly lost. Hobbes found me and showed me the way back, then left me at the powder room door. When I got back to the library,

Edgar had returned and was drinking heavily again, and not long after that Robert came back too."

"And how much time had passed between Harriet returning and you all being back in the library?"

"You think Harriet was the last one to see her alive?" I asked.

"Either her or the killer, and at the moment they could both be one and the same. There's nothing to indicate how long it took for Harriet to come back after the argument. Was it straight away? Or did she follow Miss Ludere into the garden, strangle her and return to the library with a fabricated story of an argument? Or did the argument take place, but earlier than she indicated to you?"

"I can't help with the time, Albert, I was out of the library as well and was gone for a good fifteen minutes. Edgar had already returned by the time I did and any one of them could have left and returned a second time before I got back."

"Well, we'll ask them all during the interview stage. I needed to get your information first."

"There is something else. When I got lost … " I had no time to finish what I was going to say as there was an abrupt knock at the door and Mortimer came in, holding up an envelope.

"Ella." He nodded to me then spoke to Albert, "We've just found this in the hand of the deceased, Albert. Casts rather a different light on things I think."

I stood up and approached as Albert tipped out the contents onto a small side table. It was a shirt button, a monogrammed shirt button to be precise.

"We'll need the shirt."

"Baxter's already on it," said Mortimer. "Gone to check both gentlemen's closets and the laundry room. He'll find it."

I looked again at the small button and the subtle letter R engraved in the centre, and wondered which of the two men it belonged to.

We didn't have long to wait as with a short rat-a-tat at the door Baxter entered, with not only the shirt, but its owner.

Mortimer left while Baxter took up position by the door so I remained quietly on the window seat while Albert spoke.

"Please take a seat," Albert said.

"I'd rather stand. What's the meaning of this?"

"It's not a request, Mr. Rutherford. Sit down."

Edgar shot a nervous glance at me, all bravado vanishing in an instant at Albert's tone and did as he was told.

"Look, Commissioner—"

Albert held up a hand. "Mr. Rutherford, let me explain how this interview is going to progress. I will ask the questions and you will provide the answers. Understood? At no time while I am speaking are you to interrupt me. You will be given an opportunity to give me your side of the story and to defend yourself afterward."

"Defend?" Edgar said in a hoarse whisper.

Albert ignored him. "Mr. Rutherford, take a good look at this shirt. Is it yours?"

Edgar looked at the shirt on the table and nodded. "Yes."

"You're quite sure?"

"Yes, of course, my buttons are monogrammed."

"And is this the shirt you were wearing last night?"

"It is."

Albert made a great show of writing in his note book, taking his time while Edgar sat nervously shaking his leg and running his hand through his hair.

"Tell me about the argument you and Miss Ludere had in the garden last night, please."

"What? What argument?"

"I would advise you to not take me for an idiot, Mr. Rutherford," Albert said sternly.

Edgar waved his hand in the air and leant back in the chair.

"It was nothing. I went to see if she was all right, that's all. She'd had a bit to drink at dinner and looked a little worse for wear."

"And was she pleased to see you?"

"No, actually she wasn't. But you obviously know all this otherwise you wouldn't be asking."

"I'd like to hear it in your own words, Mr. Rutherford. Please continue."

"She was on her way to the powder room when I met up with her. I was going for some fresh air and asked her to join me."

"And how did she seem, apart from a little drunk?"

"Annoyed actually, though I didn't know why then. Anyway I left and walked along the front of the house trying to clear my head. I'd almost reached the corner when I heard her behind me. I could tell she was angry immediately. She'd had some row with that librarian, put her in a god-awful mood."

I let out a shaky breath as I realised Edgar's words had not only confirmed Harriet's story, but had possibly put her in the clear.

"And what was the argument about?"

"Patty-Mae seemed to think she was trying to steal Robert away from her." Edgar let out a humourless laugh. "As if she could. I mean, why the hell would Robert be interested in some dowdy, frumpy, antiquated fossil when he was going to marry her? She was being a stupid little fool and I told her so."

I clenched my fists and bit my tongue so I wouldn't give him a piece of my mind. Goodness, how I disliked this horrible shallow man.

There was silence. Albert looked up from his scribblings, but Edgar remained mute.

"What happened then, Mr. Rutherford?"

"Nothing."

"Nothing? You mean to tell me the victim, not only drunk, but furious after a row with Miss Dinworthy, came to you only to be told she was a stupid little fool, and nothing else happened? Perhaps you're assuming I'm also a fool, Mr. Rutherford?" Albert said coldly.

"No. No, of course not. Look, if I tell you, it's not what it sounds like. It was just—I'm sorry, I can't." Edgar jumped up from his chair in a state of agitation.

"Sit down, Mr. Rutherford. Do you recognise this?"

Albert took the envelope containing the button and emptied it onto the table. Edgar peered at it, a frown marring his face.

"Yes, it's one of my buttons. But where … ?"

"Is there a button missing from this shirt, the one you have stated is yours and which you were wearing last night?"

Edgar cautiously lifted the shirt and examined it carefully.

"Yes, the right cuff button is missing. I didn't realise I'd lost it."

"Would you like to know where that button was found, Mr. Rutherford?"

Edgar looked up and gulped audibly, but didn't answer.

"It was found in the hand of the victim."

Edgar moaned and began to sob.

"I didn't kill her. Please, you have to believe me. I would never hurt Patty-Mae."

"Then how did the button of your shirt end up in her hand?"

"She hit me. Slapped me across the face when I insulted her. She was furious, like a wild animal. She kept hitting me over and over, pulling my shirt and calling me names. I had to hold her wrists to stop her, but then she started kicking. It was like she was possessed or something. I couldn't stop her. I must have lost the button then."

He was sobbing like a child, furiously wiping his nose and eyes on his sleeve. It was pitiful to watch and I honestly didn't know how much more I could take.

"You did nothing to defend yourself? Come now, this woman was hitting you, kicking you and calling you names as though possessed, you said. I could see easily how you would be provoked to anger. Is that what happened, Edgar? Did you hit her harder than you meant to? Was it an accident which, when you realised what you'd done, you made look like a murder?"

Albert's voice had softened. Gone was the harsh Police Commissioner and in his place a sympathetic friend.

"No!" Edgar wailed. "Please, that's not how it happened. Eventually her anger fizzled out," he hiccuped through sobs. "She told me to bugger off, so I did. I left and went back inside, but she was alive when I left her, I swear she was."

"You mean you let her get away with it? You didn't hit her once? I find that very hard to believe, Edgar. Are you sure? Just think back to last night and tell me what really happened. I'm here to help you, Edgar."

Albert's voice was hypnotic as he tried to coax the truth from an increasingly hysterical Edgar.

"Dammit! Just once. I slapped her, but only once. She was hysterical! It was the only thing I could do to calm her down, shock her back to reality. But I didn't kill her."

I hadn't seen Albert signal Baxter, but he came over, handcuffs at the ready.

"Edgar Rutherford, I am arresting you for the murder of Miss Patty-Mae Ludere," said Albert, standing.

"What? No! Please, I didn't do it! You have the wrong man. Whoever did it has set me up."

He wrestled himself away from Baxter and was heading for the door, but Baxter was too quick for him. Tackling him to the ground, Baxter placed one knee on his back, grabbed his arms up behind him and in a flash had him trussed up like a turkey.

"On your feet, lad, don't make it worse for yourself," Baxter said gruffly, hauling Edgar upright.

Edgar took a step toward me. "Ella, please, I didn't do it. Please keep snooping. Find out who did kill her because he's still around. Please, Ella, please help me. I didn't kill Patty-Mae. I couldn't."

He then broke down in sobs as Baxter led him out of the room and to the waiting police car.

Mortimer came to stand with us and watched as Edgar was taken away.

"Looks like you got your man then, Albert?" he said.

Albert nodded thoughtfully.

But I wasn't so sure.

CHAPTER EIGHTEEN

lbert and I walked back into the foyer of Arundel Hall, both deep in thought.

"Ella, I want you to do as Mr. Rutherford suggested and keep snooping," he said quietly.

I looked at him in astonishment.

"You don't think he killed her?"

"I'm reserving judgment at this stage, but my gut says not. However, there's certainly more to all this than meets the eye and that young man knows more than he's saying."

"But why arrest him if you don't think he's guilty?"

"I didn't say he wasn't guilty. He most certainly is guilty of something. If not the murder, then something associated with it. Let him stew for a while. This way he'll have time to consider his actions and his character.

I expect he'll find himself wanting on both scores. And it may very well flush the real culprit out into the open."

"Albert, how did you know Edgar had slapped Patty-Mae?"

"Apart from the reasons I mentioned when questioning him, you mean?"

I nodded.

"Mortimer informed me there was the marking of a hand print across her left cheek. She died not long afterward, so it was still visible."

"Is it true, Commissioner? You've arrested that young scoundrel for the murder of my poor Patty-Mae?"

Sir Robert came shuffling up the hall looking years older than he had when I'd first arrived. The dandy had gone and he was once more an old country gentleman dressed in his tweeds. But his pallor was sallow and the lines in his face accentuated. He looked wretched. Behind him stood Harriet and Nathaniel, eyes unnaturally bright and restless with the expectation of news.

"Mr. Rutherford has just been taken into custody, Sir Robert, yes."

"Thank god. I hope he hangs," he said vehemently. "I suppose I should sort out the funeral arrangements."

Albert stepped forward and laying a hand on Robert's shoulder, spoke quietly. "Sir Robert, might I suggest you wait a few days? There are still some loose ends we need to tie up, and until those are concluded, Patty-Mae will need to remain with my colleagues in London. I'm sure you understand. I'll telephone you as soon as I know when she can be released."

"Yes, all right, Commissioner. But don't drag it out. I don't think I could bear it."

As Robert slowly departed, Nathaniel approached. "Does this mean we're allowed to leave, Commissioner?"

"Not just yet, Doctor Brookes. I'd still like to speak to you and Miss Dinworthy. Come to the drawing room in ten minutes please. Miss Dinworthy, we'll call for you shortly."

Harriet nodded in response.

Ten minutes later, Doctor Brookes entered the drawing room, holding the door for Mrs. Shaw who had thoughtfully provided afternoon tea for us.

"So what's all this about, Commissioner? I thought the perpetrator had been caught and the case closed."

"As I said to Sir Robert, there are a number of loose ends I wish to tie up to my satisfaction before I close the case. Can you tell me your movements after you left the dinner table last night?"

"I left with Harriet. We had a brief chat in the hall about the library and her published works, then we went our separate ways. It took me a short while to find the gentleman's facilities. I used them, then went back to the library for coffee, where I found Ella with a rather upset Harriet. When Ella left, Harriet asked if I had something to soothe her nerves, so I went to the car to pick up my bag. When I got back, Harriet was still seated by the fire, so we waited together until everyone returned. Edgar came back first and promptly grabbed a bottle of brandy, then Ella and finally Robert. After that we searched for a hidden door and found the cellars."

"Did you hear the argument between Miss Ludere and Harriet?"

"Ah, so that's why she was upset? I didn't realise. No, I never heard a thing."

"And when you went to get your bag, did you see Miss Ludere at all?"

"No. The car had been taken around the back to the stable block. It's at the opposite side of the building to where she was found, so I wouldn't have seen her. I used the door at that side to leave and return."

"Nathaniel," I said, gathering my courage, "When I asked if you knew Patty-Mae you said no."

"I don't. Sorry, didn't."

"But when we arrived she was exceptionally rude to you. I don't think she liked you very much, but how could that be? It's hardly the way you'd treat a stranger."

Nathaniel rose and sauntered to look out of the window, hands in his pockets. Albert and I shared a glance and waited for him to speak. He was obviously wrestling with his conscience and I was intrigued as to what he was going to say. Eventually he made up his mind and turned to face us, leaning against the wall with his arms folded.

"As a doctor I'm bound by certain laws and ethics when it comes to confidentiality."

"Was Miss Ludere a patient of yours?" asked Albert.

"Not as such no, but I don't suppose it matters if I tell you now she's dead. In all honesty I was planning on going to the police anyway. I wanted to do a little detective work of my own first though."

"Of course, the note in your bag," I exclaimed. "PM Police. I thought you had an evening visit with the police, but I see now PM stood for Patty-Mae, not post meridiem."

"Ella, you searched my doctor's bag?" Nathaniel was surprised, but seemed to be more amused than angry.

"No, of course I didn't. When you came to see me about my wrist and fell that day, all the contents scattered everywhere. I put everything back, but I couldn't help but notice the note. I certainly wasn't snooping."

Nathaniel laughed. "Not one of my finer moments."

Albert cleared his throat. "Please, go on with your story, Doctor Brookes."

"Patty-Mae came to see me a few days ago, accosted me actually on my doorstep one night. It was pitch black and well after hours and I was returning home from an emergency house visit. I was just putting my key in the lock and suddenly there she was. Practically jumped out of the privet and gave me a terrible start, I can tell you."

"What did she want?" I asked.

"Drugs," Nathaniel said simply. "She had an addiction to opiates and had run out. Apparently the chap who usually supplied her, and don't ask me who it was because I don't know, was in a bit of trouble, got himself into debt and no one was prepared to give him any more credit. I of course refused point blank. Even if I could have helped her, it's not something I would have done. Unfortunately she turned quite nasty when I refused. She'd been drinking and became belligerent and abusive, but I stuck to my guns and eventually she left. That was the one and only time I had met her until last night. Of course, I was aware of who she was. You can't live in a small village like this and not hear the rumours."

"Was she wearing heels?" I asked.

Both men stared at me as though I'd gone quite potty.

"Bear with me. Well?"

"Yes, she was actually. I remember because she damn near broke her ankle in her rush to leave."

"And this was at your surgery?" asked Albert.

Nathaniel shook his head. "No, actually, it was at my home. Surgery hours were over."

I knew roughly where Nathaniel lived and it wasn't easy to get to. It was off an obscure little road, which unless you knew it was there you would miss entirely. It would take the knowledge of a local to find it, which Patty-Mae was not.

"Gentlemen, if you'll excuse me just one minute," I said and dashed out the door.

"Hobbes?" I called.

"Yes, Miss?" a voice inquired from behind my left shoulder.

How did he do that?

"Hobbes, do you know if Miss Ludere drove a motor car?"

"I do, and she didn't. She preferred to be chauffeur driven and had never sat behind a wheel herself."

"Thank you, Hobbes, you've been very helpful," I said, returning to the drawing room. "I've just spoken with Hobbes and Patty-Mae didn't know how to drive. She was in high heels when she came to see you, Nathaniel, and it was at your house not the surgery, which is difficult enough to get to by car, let alone walk."

"So she must have had a friend with her," Nathaniel said. "Someone who drove and knew where to find me. I can't see Robert doing it, so it must have been some-one else."

"Exactly. And her main friend on the island, one who would know where you live, Nathaniel, is ... "

"Mr. Rutherford," finished Albert. "Very interesting."

"And something else interesting, Albert. I overheard an argument the other day between an insalubrious gen-tleman, most definitely a thug, and another younger, well-spoken man at the rear of the King's Head. The young man was being quite seriously threatened due to a significant debt. I thought nothing more of it. To tell you the truth, it was none of my business. But when Edgar arrived here, I recognised his voice straight away. He was the one in trouble."

"Well, it seems I have a lot of questions to ask Mr. Rutherford," said Albert. "Doctor Brookes, is there anything more? No? Well, if you'd be so kind as to ask Miss Dinworthy to come in, you're also free to go home. However, I may need to speak with you again."

"Of course, Commissioner, you know where to find me. Ella, I'll telephone you tomorrow," Nathaniel said and left.

CHAPTER NINETEEN

Harriet entered, looking very smart. She'd changed into a tweed skirt and jacket the colour of moorland heathers, and the soft lilacs and purples suited her tremendously. A small gold filigree brooch in the shape of a rose was pinned at the throat of her soft cream blouse and she'd done her hair. But most surprisingly, she was wearing lipstick. It was a soft pink colour, very delicate and barely noticeable, but I had never seen her wearing cosmetics of any kind.

"Ah, Miss Dinworthy, please do take a seat," Albert said graciously.

"Now, as you have no doubt heard, there are some details I would like to go over in order to tie up some loose ends. Could you tell me what you did after dinner last night?"

Harriet nodded. Settling back in the chair, she crossed her feet at the ankles and clasped her hands neatly in her lap.

"I left the dining room with Doctor Brookes. After a little conversation we parted company and I went to the powder room. When I entered, I found Miss Ludere was there. She was reapplying her lipstick, rather unsteadily I might add, and gave me such a venomous look I was quite taken aback. I had met the woman precisely once before and couldn't understand initially why she would obviously hate me so much. It was craven, I know, but I deliberately took my time using the facilities in the hope she would leave, but unfortunately she had waited for me."

"I hardly think wanting to avoid a confrontation is a sign of cowardice, Harriet," I said.

"Well, perhaps you're right, Isobella. However, I'm afraid when cornered I come out fighting, and regrettably that's just what I did last night. Not physically, you understand, but verbally, and by the time I had finished she was furious. A few unvarnished truths and having a mirror held up to you will do that. It's not something I'm proud of and I was quite shaken and upset afterward, but I wasn't prepared to stand by and be spoken to like that."

"And what exactly did Miss Ludere say to you?" asked Albert.

"I'm sure Isobella has brought you up to date, Commissioner, but if you insist. She quite simply told me to stay away from Robert. That after the party was over I was to sever all contact with him. She said with my feelings for him I was a threat to her marriage and her happy life. All nonsense of course and I refused. Robert and I have been friends all our lives and I wasn't going to be dictated to by the likes of Miss Ludere, who in my opinion was in this relationship for one thing and one thing only, money."

"But Patty-Mae's accusations and concerns weren't all nonsense were they, Harriet?" I asked softly.

"My dear Isobella, as sharp as always. Well, I don't suppose there's any point in denying it. I loved Robert, I still do. When we were young, it was assumed we would marry. Of course life conspired against us. Robert left when war broke out and when he returned, he was married. I was shocked and heartbroken of course. I'd waited, you see, and for me there was no other. But the atrocities of war change people and Robert had seen much in his service.

"But life goes on and I slowly mended by throwing myself into studying, then teaching, then writing. My work was and still is a lifeline, and I've been lucky enough to be successful in my chosen field. I have no regrets apart from the obvious one, but I couldn't stand aside and watch while Robert was hoodwinked by a gold-digger. I told her in no uncertain terms what I thought of her, but I didn't kill her as you now know, nor could I have done. But I can't say I'm sorry she no longer has her claws set into Robert."

"You've been very candid, Miss Dinworthy, in what was obviously a difficult and emotional telling and I appreciate your honesty. I think I have all I need from you, but will call again if questions crop up. You are of course free to return home," said Albert.

"Actually, Robert has asked me to stay on and I have agreed. It's a difficult time for him to be alone and he needs a friend."

Ah, I thought, *that explains the lipstick and the extra care she's taken with her appearance.* I was happy for her. After several decades apart, perhaps they could find love and companionship together in their twilight years. I also fervently hoped the curse wouldn't rear its ugly head and thwart their chances.

"Oh, isn't it wonderful to be home, Mrs. Shaw?" I said as we entered the cottage and laid our cases in the hall. "I know it's only been a short while, but it has felt like a lifetime with all that's gone on."

"It is indeed, Miss Bridges. I for one shall be glad to get to my own bed. Not that the accommodation at Arundel Hall wasn't good, but I won't miss the snores of Mrs. Butterworth, God bless her heart. I was amazed the roof was still on this morning. Now, shall I make you a pot of tea and a small supper before I retire?"

"That would be most welcome, Mrs. Shaw, thank you. I'll light the fire in the sitting room and eat in there," I told her. But first I wanted to check something.

I followed her downstairs and while she put away her bags, I slipped into the pantry. Taking the torch from a shelf, I opened the secret door and moving down to the far end I shone the torch at the chair.

"Oh, no. I thought you would have left by now," I said to the apparition in front of me.

I was sure I had solved her mystery, but perhaps I was wrong and there was something else I needed to do. However, if that was the case, I didn't know what it could be. More disturbingly though, she carried a black cat in her arms, the one I'd come to think of as my own. Dear Phantom. Had he belonged to her so many years ago? Had he appeared to me purely seeking justice for his mistress?

She gave me a small bow of her head and raised her hand. I watched as she gradually faded, then disappeared completely, taking my feline friend with her.

It was a bittersweet moment. She was free and had obviously waited to say goodbye. I had solved the mystery, after all, but she'd taken Phantom with her and I found a lump in my throat at the thought I would never see him again. For a ghost cat, who appeared at will and was rarely solid, he had certainly wormed his way into my heart.

I left and climbed the steps back to the sitting room, sniffing and blinking tears from my eyes.

"Not catching a cold I hope, Miss Bridges?" Mrs. Shaw said as she laid out my supper tray.

"Nothing like that, just a bit of dust from the downstairs dining room. I think the pantry can be restocked now. Tom Parsons is due to start work in the morning. Perhaps you could ask him to help? Also I think he could be trusted to lay the fires too, it will save you a job."

"Very well. Good night, Miss Bridges."

"Good night, Mrs. Shaw."

As I sat and stared into the flames, my mind went over the events of the last twenty-four hours. The fire was more of an extravagance than a necessity as it wasn't particularly cold, but I found it both comforting and relaxing.

I'd felt considerably put out when Albert had informed me I wouldn't be there to help interview Robert.

"Sir Robert doesn't want you to be present, I'm afraid, Ella, and I will respect his wishes. I believe he'll be more forthcoming with me alone," he'd said.

"But that's ridiculous, Albert. I can sit in the background and not speak if you'd prefer. He won't even know I'm there."

But Albert wouldn't budge. Robert was old fashioned in his beliefs and didn't think it was the place for a woman, let alone a 'young chit of a girl'. Albert had said he would make copious notes. "And I'll come and see you at the cottage tomorrow to let you know what was said," he'd promised.

"Well, don't forget to ask him about his visitor," and I went on to confirm how Hobbes had called Robert out from the library, how I'd got lost and inadvertently overheard a partial conversation, then Robert's account when he'd returned.

"There might very well be a perfectly reasonable explanation, but it struck me as odd at the time, and I think it's worth investigating a little more."

Now, a few hours later, and sat alone in my cottage, I wondered how the conversation between Robert and Albert was playing out up at The Hall. I suspected it was all very genial over a brandy and a cigar or two in front of the library fire. Two men chatting as though at their club. No wonder there was no place for me.

Sighing, I spent a little time on Aunt Margaret's latest puzzle to take my mind off them. It was a particularly ingenious one and without my trusted little dictionary to hand and my eyes blurring with fatigue, I barely managed to complete half of it. Too tired to concentrate, I tamped down the fire and went up to bed. Tomorrow was going to be a busy day.

CHAPTER TWENTY

Several things happened at once the next morning. I'd just finished breakfast when Mrs. Shaw came to inform me Tom Parsons was at the door. "With his dog," she said with a disapproving sniff.

I was halfway down the back stairs when the telephone rang, then just before I picked up the receiver the front door bell chimed.

"My word, it's like Piccadilly Circus here this morning," said Mrs. Shaw as she went to answer the door.

"Hello, Linhay…"

"Ella, good morning, it's Nathaniel," the deep voice said before I could finish. "I just wanted to make sure you got home all right."

"I did, yes, thank you, Nathaniel. Sorry, could you excuse me one moment?"

I looked at my housekeeper who was hovering behind me.

"Sorry to interrupt, Miss Bridges, but Sir Arthur Montesford is here. Shall I show him to the drawing room?"

"Put him in the small sitting room please, Mrs. Shaw, I'll not be long."

Turning back to the telephone, I said, "Nathaniel, I'm sorry, but Albert has just arrived. Could I call you back?"

"Yes, of course, although I'll be out and about most of the day, so the evening will be best."

After hanging up, I went to see Albert to explain I needed to see Tom, but I'd not be a moment. "In the meantime, help yourself to coffee," I said, indicating the tray Mrs. Shaw had deposited in front of him.

Down in the kitchen, I greeted Tom warmly, patted Digger on the head and explained Mrs. Shaw would be looking after him, but I would be back down to see him if I could before he left for the day.

Back upstairs I went to the sitting room and joined Albert in a cup of coffee and asked him how it had gone at The Hall.

"It was as you suspected, Ella," Albert said, adding cream and four heaped teaspoons of sugar to his coffee as well as another inch to his ever-expanding girth.

"It was nothing to do with escaped sheep, rather a painting he wished to purchase as a wedding present for Miss Ludere. She'd seen it in London apparently and fallen for it. He'd got this fellow Entwhistle to investigate it for him, check the provenance and so forth and it turned out to be a fake."

"And what about the other man I heard them mention?"

"Another buyer who was interested. Robert wanted to make sure he was successful in the purchase, didn't want any competition. But as it was a fake it was a moot point."

"But why make up some silly story about sheep?"

"He didn't want to let the cat out of the bag. It was to be a surprise gift and he didn't want anyone to accidentally spill the beans. Remember, he also didn't know where Miss Ludere was at the time and didn't want her to overhear. As simple as that really."

"But, Albert," I said, not willing to let it go, "does it not strike you as rather an odd time for this Entwhistle man to be calling? It was late, we'd just finished dinner."

"Robert is a wealthy man, Ella. I daresay he can demand people work all hours if he pays them enough. He wanted to know as soon as possible and told Entwhistle so. Entwhistle took him literally and so turned up as soon as he'd garnered the information."

"It would have been much easier to telephone," I muttered, sipping my coffee.

"Of course it would, but Robert's the sort of man who doesn't trust telephones. Ears listening in and all that. No, he asked for a report in person and that's what he got."

"So you're just taking what he said at face value?" I asked.

Albert gave me a combined stern and semi-amused look over the rim of his coffee cup. "You should know me better than that, Ella. I have a man checking his story at the gallery where the painting is located."

"Of course, I apologise, Albert. I felt rather peeved when I wasn't included last night and I'm being a bit crotchety about it. Just ignore me. I'm over it now. Are you going back to London today?"

"I am. I need to speak with young Rutherford again. Why? Do you want to tag along?"

"May I?"

"You may. I'd like you present when I speak to Edgar actually. He seems to trust you."

I chuckled. "I doubt that very much, but he considers me a snoop of the first order, and if he is telling the truth when he says he had nothing to do with the death of Patty-Mae, then I think he'll be more forthcoming in his answers if I'm there."

"Well, shall we say half an hour then?"

I'll go and tell Mrs. Shaw I'll be out for the day and to look after Tom and his dog."

Thirty minutes later, I was seated in Albert's splendid motor car leaving the island behind for the hustle and bustle of the capital. And the alien world of a prison cell.

I had never before set foot in Scotland Yard, although I had seen the building many times, located as it was upon Victoria Embankment. An imposing Victorian Romanesque style structure, built in banded red brick and white Portland stone on a base of granite, it was built on land reclaimed from the River Thames. Ironically during construction, the dismembered torso of a woman was found by workers, and the case was never solved.

Albert drove to the rear of the building and we entered through a small unobtrusive door painted bottle green, beyond which a set of stone steps led down to a basement.

"Apologies for using the 'tradesman's entrance', Ella. I find it preferable to come in unannounced on occasion."

At the foot of the stairs a wood panel door with a round glass window showed a corridor beyond bustling with life, and this was where Albert led me.

A couple of men in white coats jostled against others in suits and ties, who in turn rubbed shoulders and shouted jocular greetings to uniformed officers. All spoke or nodded to Albert with the deference awarded to him by rank, but gave me openly puzzled looks or surreptitious glances, not quite able to label me one thing or another. Was I a suspect, a witness or something more? And what was I doing in such exalted company? I doubt anyone would have believed I was consulting on a murder case.

"Good morning, Commissioner, and Miss Bridges, what a pleasant surprise. What brings you to the bowels of the yard?"

"Hello, Mortimer," Albert said. "Ella's helping me out with the Arundel Hall case. We're here to have another talk with young Rutherford."

"Well, if you have time, please do call up to the laboratory, Ella. I'd like to show you around our latest forensic techniques. I'm sure you'll find it interesting."

"Thank you. Certainly, if time allows, I'd very much like to visit," I said.

"And, Albert, I finished my report with regard to Miss Ludere. You'll find it on your desk."

Albert and I took our leave of Mortimer and descended another staircase, this one leading to the holding cells where prisoners were kept prior to being sentenced, or drunks picked up in the night lay sleeping it off. Through the door, a uniformed constable sat at a scarred table reading the paper. He jumped up sharpish when Albert pushed open the door and thrust a clipboard out for him to sign.

"Thank you, sir. Will you be needing an interview room, sir?"

"Not this time, constable. Has Mr. Rutherford contacted a solicitor, do you know?"

"He has, sir. According to the docket," the constable checked one of numerous official looking forms on the board, "he should be here in about an hour, sir."

"Well, that should give us enough time, thank you, constable. Oh, and please bring two chairs to cell twelve."

The atmosphere as we walked on was dismal in the extreme, with an overpowering smell of human waste and unwashed bodies, mixed with cleaning fluid and lye soap. It took all of my willpower, and a handkerchief over my nose and mouth, to prevent me from gagging. It was also very cold. The narrow corridor was stone underfoot with a brick arched ceiling and brick walls, and every step echoed around our heads and bounced back to assault our ears.

The brick was painted in what originally would have been a soft cream, but now bore dubious stains and the grime of years, which mottled it to a sickly dark yellow. There were twelve cells in total, six to a side and each one no bigger than a broom closet.

They contained identical cots covered in thin grey woollen blankets and a bucket in the opposite corner. The only light came from a small arched window set high in the wall and faced with bars. Only three of the cells were occupied. One held what looked at first glance to be a bunch of rags on the cot, but was in fact a vagrant. Brought in for being drunk and disorderly the night before, according to Albert. He would soon be turned out to begin the cycle again, and no doubt would find himself a bed for tonight in the same place.

The second cell, opposite the beggar, was occupied by a huge, terrifying individual with a mass of dirty black hair and only one eye. A vivid puckered scar running from hairline to chin spoke of how he'd lost the other. His single orb glared at me with black malevolence and I hurried past the gated door to his cell to the accompaniment of jeers and laughter, and the aggressive rattling of bars.

The third cell at the farthest end and well away from the others housed Edgar.

As soon as we came into sight he jumped up, eyes wild and desperate, and clung to the bars. "Thank god. Have you news? Have you caught the killer?"

Albert glanced at me and remained silent.

"Edgar, there's been little progress, but there is something that's come to light, which we need to ask you about," I said.

At that moment the constable came dragging two remarkably uncomfortable-looking wooden chairs behind him. We thanked him, positioned them a few feet from the front of Edgar's cell door and sat.

"Edgar, did you take Patty-Mae to visit Doctor Brookes the other night?"

"Yes."

"Why?"

"Because she asked me to. She didn't drive a motor car."

"Edgar, you know very well that's not what I meant. Why did Patty-Mae need to see the doctor?"

"I don't know, she never said."

And there it was, that little sign Aunt Margaret had told me to watch out for.

"Edgar, you are lying to me. I'm here to try and help you, at your request I might add, but if you're going to lie then there's not much point in my being here."

I stood up to leave.

"No, wait. She needed drugs. She had an addiction. I tried to help her, but it was no good. She just couldn't do without it."

It was at that moment I realised just what I'd heard between Edgar and the man who had threatened him at The King's Head.

"It was you who was procuring the drugs for her, wasn't it? But of course she couldn't pay you for them and now you're in debt and a lot of trouble as a result. Why did you do it, Edgar, out of friendship? No of course not. It was because you loved her, didn't you?"

This was pure guesswork on my part, but I couldn't think what else it could be. I prayed I was right and waited for a response.

Edgar sat on the cot and put his head in his hands and wept.

"Edgar, do you realise how much trouble you're in?" I asked softly. "If you're found guilty then you will hang. Why would you want to hang for a murder you did not commit? I will try to help you, Edgar, but you must tell me what happened."

He sat up, wiping his eyes and nose on the back of his hand and began to speak in a monotone, eyes unfocused and staring ahead as though recalling a visual memory.

"I was getting the drugs from someone in London. I'd sold a few things to get the money and it was all working out fine for a while. But then Patty-Mae wanted more and more and eventually I ran out of things to sell. So I started getting it on credit using different suppliers and paying off bits when I could. Eventually the word got out I couldn't pay and every door was slammed in my face. People came after me, threatening to break my legs, or worse. So I ran back to Linhay and kept my head down. Patty-Mae had enough to last a couple of weeks and then she ran out. She was getting desperate and I didn't know where else to go. I couldn't go back to London, I'd have been killed on the spot and my body thrown in the Thames. So as a last resort I took her to Doctor Brookes. No doubt he's told you he refused to help."

I glanced at Albert who'd been making notes in his little black book from the moment we'd sat down. He made a motion with his hand for me to continue, but didn't interrupt.

"Edgar, you introduced Robert to Patty-Mae. How did you feel when they fell in love and decided to marry? It must have hurt a great deal."

"Have you ever been on the wrong end of unrequited love, Ella? Well, that was how it was with Patty-Mae. She never loved me, barely knew I existed except to provide her with her drug."

I sighed and got up, moving closer to the bars.

"How am I supposed to help you if you won't tell me the truth? Perhaps I should tell you some truths to make you see how serious this is."

I began to count the points on my fingers.

"Number one, so far you are the only one in the frame for the murder. Number two, you knew the victim well, you were friends. Number three, you've said you were in love with her, yet she didn't look upon you in the same way. Frankly, I believe that's a lie. However, all it does is add more ammunition to the case against you. Number four, you supplied her with drugs and got into debt and danger because of it. Number five, by your own admission you had a violent argument on the night she was killed. Number six, your shirt button was found in her dead hand, and number seven, because thus far there is no evidence to the contrary, you were the last person to see her alive. Do you see what this means, Edgar? You had both the opportunity and more than one motive to murder Patty-Mae."

"But I didn't do it," he shouted.

"Then why are you lying?" I shouted back. "What are you hiding?"

I couldn't believe I'd raised my voice, but I was frustrated beyond belief. I couldn't understand why Edgar was being such an obstinate fool when his life was hanging in the balance. But If I'd thought my shouting and laying out of the facts would shock him into telling me the truth, I was sadly wrong.

"I can't, Ella," he said in a quiet shaky voice. "Please, just keep looking, I beg of you. I didn't kill Patty-Mae, I couldn't. I truly did love her. But I've told you all I can."

Turning away, he curled up on the cot facing the wall and would speak no more.

"Edgar, I can't begin to understand your reluctance to speak," I said to his back, "but if you change your mind, you can get word to me through the commissioner and I'll return."

On my way out I called in briefly to let Mortimer know I wouldn't be able to join him, and he assured me the invitation was always open. To be honest I felt wrung out after my visit to Edgar. It had been far more emotionally tiring, confrontational and disheartening than I'd imagined and all I wanted to do was curl up in front of the fire at home and sleep.

Albert, ever gracious, had offered to drive me back to Linhay, but I'd refused. I wanted to be alone for a while, and the perfect place for me to restore my wits and my equilibrium would be on the train. He insisted on driving me to the station, which I gladly accepted. Being jostled in the crowded city streets held no appeal at all. In my exhausted state I could very well find myself under a bus.

"That was an excellent interview, Ella. I doubt very much I could have done better myself. I'm intrigued as to how you knew he was lying? That sort of skill would be deuced useful to The Yard."

"It was my Aunt Margaret who taught me. I spent some time living with her and she showed me what to look for. She is a puzzle expert and an avid people watcher. Over the years she put together a lot of clues and the result was various signs to look for when people are being less than truthful."

"So it's a teachable skill?"

"Yes. I said to her once she should write a book about it, but she said she was too long in the tooth to start such a project, that sort of thing was for the younger generation, plus she thought it would take all the fun out of it."

"And have you thought of taking up that particular mantle? Not for the public market, of course, otherwise every criminal in the country will have the advantage, but perhaps for law enforcement officers. It could work very well in conjunction with some classroom type training."

"Dear Albert," I laughed. "That was far from subtle, even for you. Perhaps you'll give me time to think about it? I'm barely coherent at present, but I'm not discounting the idea of a manual to help with training your policemen.

It is rather a good idea actually, and one I'll give some serious thought to. But later."

"And that's all I can ask, my dear. Although there is another thing I would like you to consider. I'd like to take you on in an official capacity, as a consultant, you understand. There will be remuneration involved for your time and expenses of course. You've shown immense intuition in the cases we've been involved in together, but in this one in particular and I'd like you to be part of my team. Will you think about it?"

In all honesty I didn't need to think about it. Never before had I felt so worthwhile, so alive, as though I were contributing to something that mattered while doing something I was actually good at.

"My answer is yes, Albert. I would very much like to be part of your team, and thank you for not only asking me, but for having the faith in me to do the job."

"Well, that's excellent news. I'll get the ball rolling when I get back to the office. I'm due to see the Home Secretary this evening anyway, so I'll discuss it with him then."

"Lord Carrick?" I asked in shock. This was most unexpected. I hadn't spoken with him since his awful visit when John had died and he'd told me I needed to move out of my home and start life again under my maiden name.

"Of course. The department falls under the jurisdiction of the Home Office so naturally he'll need to be informed. Why? Is there a problem?"

I thought about it, then smiled inwardly. I would love to be a fly on the wall when Albert informed Lord

Carrick I was to be taken on as a consultant detective, and in the murder division no less. How far I had come from the naive little woman he'd patronised, pitied and lied to a few years before.

"Actually I see no problem, Albert. No problem at all."

We'd reached the train station and Albert parked the car, then walked with me into the building.

"Is there anything you'd like to add to the case, Ella, now you're officially on the payroll as it were?"

"I was thinking that perhaps we need to find out more about Patty-Mae. I for one haven't heard of her, but that means nothing. I'm neither a theatre nor movie goer, but it strikes me, and please don't take this as me telling you how to do your job, that as the victim she must have done something to warrant being killed in the first place. It seems as though we have been privy to the secrets of the others, but we still know next to nothing about the victim."

"A very good point, Ella," Albert said in such a way that I knew he'd already considered this avenue of investigation, and most probably was already in pursuit of answers. "I'll oversee those inquiries myself and will keep you updated."

I said goodbye and went to board my train, sinking into the seat with great relief. Within minutes of it setting off I was fast asleep and didn't wake again until I was back on the island.

CHAPTER TWENTY-ONE

The following morning passed quickly. Tom arrived at eight on the dot with his excitable and thoroughly enjoyable little dog, and we spent a few hours together working in the garden. The sky was a pale misty blue tinged with creamy yellow, and the sun, still low, looked like a ball of lemon sherbet, its mild warmth suffusing and loosening my limbs and boosting my sense of well-being.

Tom had already made progress through the wild thicket and brush we believed led to the walled garden, but there was still much to do. I left him to it and spent the morning trimming the roses and shrubs, cleaning and preparing tubs for spring planting, and generally pottering about. But all the while the murder case rattled around in my head, the fragmented information attempting to weld itself into some coherent whole, while the front part of my mind concentrated on more mundane matters such as compost.

At noon Tom disappeared to the kitchen for his lunch, Digger to his basket by the warm range, which I'd put there for just that purpose, and I took myself to the sitting room with a tray.

I'd barely sat down when a black shape launched itself through the window glass with barely a ripple, and landed on my desk, scattering papers hither and thither. My cat was back.

"Well, what a theatrical entrance, Phantom. I'm so glad to see you, my little feline friend. I thought you had gone for good."

Phantom gave me a haughty stare as if to say, 'you won't get rid of me that easily,' and then stretching, proceeded to curl up in the chair by the fire and fall asleep. I laughed and bent to pick up my scattered papers. As I did so, my eye caught the puzzle I'd been doing two nights before and my heart missed a beat. One word was glaring at me, not one I had filled in, but one that had automatically revealed itself as I'd filled in the other clues. In my fatigue the other night I had missed it completely. I picked it up and stared, but I had no idea what it meant, was it even English?

I dashed to the bookshelf and grabbed my little dictionary. Quickly finding the correct letter, I scanned through the entire list, but it wasn't there. Oh, why was I wasting time? A telephone call to Aunt Margaret would solve the mystery.

"Aunt Margaret, it's Ella. How are you?"

"Well, hello, my dear, I was wondering when you would call. You've solved it then?"

I always called her when I'd solved her puzzles.

"Actually no, I haven't just yet, but it is the reason I'm calling. Aunt Margaret, this is terribly important. Do you have a copy to hand?"

"Of course, but I don't need it. Whatever is the problem, Ella? You sound quite flustered."

"Can you recall seven down? What does it mean?"

"Seven down ... oh yes, one of my more ingenious clues, I thought. It's Latin, an unusual word, not much heard of nowadays of course. Unless you've studied the language you wouldn't know of it."

"So what does it mean?"

"It means bogus, Ella. Ludere is Latin for fake. Does that help, dear?"

"More than you know, Aunt Margaret."

"Can you tell me what this is all about or is it a little hush-hush?"

Astute as ever, I thought with a proud smile. "Actually, it is a little hush-hush for now, but I'll let you know as soon as I can. Thank you, Aunt Margaret, you may have helped me to solve more than just a puzzle."

"Glad to be of help, my dear, and even more so to hear you're using that brain of yours at last. Much love, darling." And she hung up.

So Patty-Mae Ludere was a fraud. I knew a puzzle clue was rather tenuous reasoning, but in my heart I knew I was right. And another thing I was almost sure of was that Edgar Rutherford knew all about it. With his education, he would be well versed in Latin. I believed this was what he refused to tell us yesterday and he'd lied about this unrequited love nonsense. Patty-Mae Ludere and Edgar Rutherford were in this together. I needed to find out why they had created such an elaborate ruse. Time to telephone Albert.

"Albert, it's Ella. Have you found out any more about Patty-Mae?"

"Nothing definitive yet, I'm sorry to say. I wired Pinkerton's Detective Agency the day following the murder, but thus far all avenues of inquiry have hit a brick wall. According to Sir Robert, she hailed from a wealthy plantation owner family in the south, but nobody down there has heard of her. It's all rather suspect."

"They won't find anything, Albert. Patty-Mae Ludere is a fake. I don't even know if she was American."

There was a lengthy pause while Albert chewed over my startling pronouncement. "How did you find out? And how sure are you, Ella?"

"As sure as I can be, and what's more, I believe Edgar knew about it. In fact, I'd be willing to bet they worked together. Although what their plan was, I don't know, but we need to talk to him again."

"I agree. How soon can you get here?"

I checked the clock in the hall. "Expect me within two hours, and Albert, could you please arrange an interview room this time. I don't think I could bear another trip to the cells."

"He's through here," Albert said, opening a door to a small gloomy room, not dissimilar to the holding cells below. Naturally there was no cot, but in the centre of the room was a scarred wooden table, with two empty chairs one side and another, occupied, opposite. A constable stood to attention next to the wall behind the prisoner.

Edgar sat with his hands on the surface, forced there by the manacles enfolding his wrists being chained through a loop in the table. He glanced up when we entered and I saw him visibly blanch at the obvious fury he saw in my face.

"So Patty-Mae was a fraud. A fake. A completely bogus persona you and she dreamed up together," I said, slapping my gloves down on the table.

Edgar was shocked. He hadn't been expecting this at all.

"How ... ?"

"How did I find out? I'm a snoop, remember, and a good one, as it turns out. Now you had better start talking, Edgar. Otherwise I'm going to leave you to rot here until it's time for the hangman to slip his noose over your neck. I'm sick to my stomach of your lying, and your misplaced martyrdom and erroneous loyalty. If it's Patty-Mae you're trying to protect, it's too late. She's dead, Edgar, and you'll be next unless you tell us everything you know. Now, who was she really and where did you meet her?"

I saw the moment in Edgar's eyes when he finally decided to tell us the truth. He was beaten and he knew it. Now all he could do was salvage what he could from the mess he had made.

"Her name was Martha Brown and I met her at a seedy little club a couple of years ago. She was ... she was one of the hostesses and also did some of the song and dance numbers. The stage was her life, it was all she'd ever wanted and if being on the stage meant she had to do a little hostess work too, then she'd do it. Her dream was to be a famous actress and singer and she was good, really good, but she just never got her break. She started in some of the better clubs and was beginning to make a name for herself when she got involved with Lucas Stamp. He'd seen her at the club and taken a fancy to her, and when Lucas wants something, he gets it," Edgar said bitterly.

Albert looked up. "Lucas Stamp, you say?"

Edgar nodded.

"Who is Lucas Stamp?" I asked.

"He is the head of organised crime in London's seedier underground. The British equivalent of a mafia crime boss with his hands in every sordid racket imaginable. From gambling to prostitution and everything in-between, including drugs," said Albert, his dark eyes like flint. "I assume he was responsible for Miss Brown's addiction?"

Again Edgar nodded. "It was his way of making her toe the line, to possess her completely and he was ruthless. Eventually, he grew tired of her and cast her aside. She lost her job at the club and with her addiction, it grew more and more difficult to find employment. She worked in eight different clubs in as many months, each one worse than the last, but she could barely function enough to do the job. Eventually she ended up in the lowest of the low, which is where I found her."

"And you became friends?" I asked, barely keeping the scepticism from my voice.

"Not at first, no. I went back several times and we started to talk. The more I got to know her, the more I realised how scared and vulnerable she was, everything else was an act. Hidden beneath the thick, poorly applied makeup, the scanty outfits and the coquettish manner, was a scared little girl and I wanted to help her, to protect her."

"So how did Martha Brown, opiate addict, hostess and dancer in a seedy London nightclub, morph into Miss Patty-Mae Ludere, celebrated American star of the silver screen?" asked Albert. "And to what purpose?"

"To be honest, I can barely remember whose idea it was. I'd taken Martha away from London. I couldn't stand the thought of her being there any longer. I took her to Linhay and put her in The Lodge. It stands empty most of the time anyway with my parents being away, and I prefer the London flat. One night I took her to see a new flick at the Granada in Tooting. I forget the star, Lombard or Garbo I think, but Martha was transfixed. At the end she said it should have been her up there on the screen, she could have done it so much better, she said, and I believed her. In the motor on the way back she recited most of the film word for word, and if I hadn't known better I could have sworn it was Garbo or Lombard sitting next to me. She was a terrific mimic. I suppose that's where the seed of the idea was planted."

"I think we will take a break there, Edgar," Albert said. "I'll have some refreshments brought in to you. Do you smoke?"

Edgar shook his head.

Albert and I left and went to his office for our own refreshments.

"So what do you think, Ella? Is he telling the truth this time?"

"Undoubtedly. It's a very raw and painful telling for him too. I wonder if Robert is aware of the deception?"

"Yes, I wonder also. It would be a first-rate motive for murder if he was. I think once we've finished here, you and I should pay another visit to Arundel Hall."

Back in the interview room, Edgar looked much better after having something to eat and a cup of tea. I also suspected sharing the weighty secret he had harboured for so long had been a huge relief.

"Please continue, Edgar. What happened next?"

"It started as a bit of fun at first. Martha wanted to put the past behind her, reinvent herself so she could appear in public, see if she could fool people. I bought her clothes and jewellery, paid for a day or two at a beauty salon and by the time she left she was barely recognisable. She practiced her make-up, copying the styles of the starlets and she practiced her accent. Before long it was second nature and Patty-Mae Ludere was born."

I asked the question I'd been pondering for a while. "Did you deliberately target Sir Robert Harlow?"

He nodded.

"Yes. What I told you before was true. Patty-Mae's addiction was costing more money than I had and I was in trouble. We both were, we needed money. She joked that if she could find herself a sugar daddy then both our troubles would be over. A few days later, I was in Robert's old bank when I overheard a couple of the ladies talking about how sad it was he'd never remarried after his wife had died. And that was that."

"But how did you know he would be attracted to her?"

He shrugged. "I didn't for sure, but Linhay is a small island and my parents and Robert became friends years ago and often attended the same London functions. It didn't take long to find a photograph of him and his wife with my mother and father. With a few tweaks ... "

"Patty-Mae modelled her look on his deceased wife," I finished for him.

Dear god, it was quite ingenious, I thought. Sly, calculating and underhand, but clever nonetheless.

"Thank you for being so candid, Edgar," Albert said. "You'll have to remain here of course, until our inquiries are complete."

"I'm probably safer here than out there anyway. Although it hardly matters. Martha is dead. I may as well be too."

"Don't be so ridiculous," I said. "Martha wouldn't want you to stop living. Besides, if what you're saying is true, her murderer is still out there and she'd want you to see justice done, I'm sure of it."

Albert and I left, but not before he'd taken the constable to one side and urged him to remove everything from Edgar's cell with which he could harm himself.

At my request, Albert escorted me to Mortimer then left to go to his office. He had rather a backlog of reports and paperwork as a result of choosing to be in the thick of this case. Under normal circumstances, it would have been assigned to a senior officer, but due to the violence and rarity of the crime, Albert had decided to become directly involved.

Mortimer was unnaturally effusive in his greeting, obviously eager to show off the department's forensic science."Now this is the area I particularly wanted to show you," said Mortimer, "The Dactyloscopy Department."

I looked at him blankly. I had no idea what he was talking about.

"Fingerprints, my dear. Fingerprints. The most significant discovery for law enforcement this century. Did you know no two fingerprints are the same? And more importantly in our field, everyone can be identified by their own?"

"Mortimer, this is astonishing," I said in genuine awe. "I had no idea things had become so advanced." Then something else occurred to me. "Mortimer, is it possible to see if there is such a print on the button from Patty-Mae's hand?"

He glanced at me quizzically. "I assume you feel Mr. Rutherford is no longer the prime suspect then? I rather thought with the button coming from his shirt, the fight he admitted to between himself and Miss Ludere, and said button being found in her hand, it was all cut and dried, so to speak?"

"I'd rather not assume anything at this stage," I said. "Personally, I feel it's all a little too obvious. I've spent several hours speaking with Edgar Rutherford and I'm now almost convinced he didn't commit the murder. If you remove him as the perpetrator then you begin to see how he could have been set up to take the blame, which is what he has maintained all along. What if someone else, the murderer, had overheard the confrontation? Say the button from his shirt had fallen to the ground during their argument, then after Patty-Mae was killed our culprit could have spied the button on the ground, picked it up and placed it in her hand. It was the perfect opportunity to throw the scent in Edgar's direction."

He nodded and smiled at me as though I were a clever pupil. I was almost surprised when he didn't pat me on the head.

"Then I shall do as you ask, my dear. However, it's a delicate procedure and as I'm sure you'll understand we only have one attempt at it. If we get it wrong during any part of the process, then this particular piece of evidence will be lost. But if we're successful then you'll need the fingerprints of the suspects in order to make a match. Let me show you how."

There followed an hour of training where Mortimer showed me how to take Exemplar prints and put them on an evidence card. It was a tricky business, and particularly messy. There were several times I smudged the card so the resulting print was useless, but eventually, after much trial and error, and blackened fingers, I got the hang of it.

"Did you take Edgar's prints or do I need to do those?"

"We already have Mr. Rutherford's prints on file. It's a mandatory procedure when bringing in a suspect. It's the others you need to obtain now. I'll get together a sampling kit to take with you."

Five minutes later, armed with my first detective kit, I went in search of Albert to tell him my plans.

"I believe this could be the break we need, Ella. Did Mortimer say how long it would take to obtain the print from the button?"

"He should have something for us tomorrow if it works. He's put it to the head of the queue."

"Then let's be on our way to Linhay. I'll telephone Doctor Brookes and we can obtain his prints first, then we can go on to Arundel Hall."

Albert drove at a much more sedate pace than was his norm on the return journey. The wind had risen during the time we were cosseted in Scotland Yard, not so apparent in the built up city streets, but once we'd hit the open road and the countryside, it buffeted the motorcar considerably.

It was already quite late and the sun was setting, its pale orb disappearing below the horizon as I watched. It would be dark by the time we arrived at Arundel Hall. Albert had decided not to call ahead. He wanted the element of surprise this time, and I wondered what sort of reception I would get. Robert had been adamant I be excluded from the initial interview. However, Albert would insist I be present this time. No more 'chit of a girl', on this occasion I was an employee of Scotland Yard.

The plan was to inform Sir Robert that through the course of our inquiries we'd discovered Patty-Mae was a fraud. Our objective was to determine whether he already knew or not and I felt sure I would be able to tell if he was lying.

"I spoke with the Home Secretary, by the way," Albert said, jarring me from my thoughts.

"And?"

"You're officially on the staff," he said, taking his eyes off the road for a minute to favour me with a smile. "However, he did take a little more persuading than I had thought."

"Because I'm a woman, you mean?"

"Not at all. Carrick's quite a progressive thinker in his way. No, it was more that I got the impression he knew your name. It was a momentary shock when I mentioned you, which he covered well, but I was intrigued."

I leant back in my seat and closed my eyes. Did I really want to open this particular Pandora's Box? Lord Carrick had insisted I would be in danger if I let slip I'd once been married to John, and so far, discounting my momentary slip on a previous case which no longer mattered as the culprits had been caught, I'd not breathed a word. The only living souls who knew were my brother Jerry, my sister-in-law Ginny, my mother and my aunt, and they also hadn't said anything. Nor had they in fact asked any questions apart from the initial ones borne of curiosity, which I'd refused to answer. But if I spoke now who knew how many complicated problems it would generate? Then again, Albert was the Commissioner of Scotland Yard, and as Ginny's godfather was almost family. If I couldn't trust him, then who could I trust? There was also a little voice in my head telling me with his connections and my new found access to Scotland Yard, I could discover more about who John really was, and that was extremely tempting.

I decided to trust my intuition and for the first time in two years spoke about my marriage, the death of my husband and the resulting visit from the Home Secretary.

"Good lord, Ella. I am sorry, I had no idea."

"Of course you didn't, there's no need to apologise. What I found most difficult was the knowledge that I had been lied to, both by John and by Lord Carrick. You must remember this was before I went to live with Aunt Margaret so she hadn't yet passed on her knowledge. But I must have had some skill even then; it was intuitive I suppose. I still don't know what sort of danger I could possibly have been in. However, that will be determined when I find out exactly who, or what, John was."

"And is your intuition telling you anything now?"

"As a matter of fact, it is. I think John may have been a spy."

CHAPTER TWENTY-TWO

Nathaniel was waiting for us in the surgery. It was well after closing time, but he'd suggested we meet him there as it was more convenient.

"So you're a detective now, Ella?" Nathaniel asked with a grin as I inked each finger and carefully transferred the prints to the two cards, one for each hand.

I smiled. "On a consultancy basis, yes."

"And you need my prints to eliminate me as a suspect, I suppose?"

"That's right, although I also need the practice. You're my first," I said, then felt myself blush at the look he gave me.

He looked down and cleared his throat. "So what of Rutherford? I thought he was your man?"

I hesitated. I didn't for one minute think Nathaniel had murdered Patty-Mae, but he was still a suspect and I needed to be circumspect regarding the information I imparted. And regardless of Albert's warning, where Nathaniel was concerned I was letting my emotions get in the way. However, before I'd had chance to think of a suitable reply, Albert answered.

"Rutherford is still in custody, Doctor Brookes. However, we need to ensure we've crossed all our 'T's' and dotted all our 'i's', as it were. There is such a thing as the 'chain of evidence', which we need to strictly adhere to."

"Of course, I understand," Nathaniel said, reaching for a small brown bottle of swabbing alcohol to remove the ink stains from his hands.

"The ink is dry now," I said. "Could you add your signature at the bottom to confirm these are your prints. And date it here, please."

Nathaniel did as I asked and I put the cards away safely in my evidence kit.

As we were leaving, Nathaniel put his hand on my arm, holding me back.

"Ella, when all this is over, would you like to go out to dinner with me? Perhaps take in a show beforehand?"

I glanced up into his handsome face and his clear, seductive eyes. "When this is over, there's nothing I'd like more, Nathaniel," I said.

The approach to The Hall was very different than the last time I had come this way, remarkably only a few short days ago. Gone were the torches and the twinkling fairy lights in the trees that cast a glow of magic and enchanted expectation; now dark and foreboding, its length seemed interminable. The statuary in the fountain was thankfully unchanged. Still no sign of the water that would add to its ghoulishness, but it looked more malevolent than ever.

Albert pulled up at the door and once again Hobbes was there to greet us.

"Commissioner, Miss Bridges. Are you expected?"

"We're not, Hobbes. If you'd like to tell Sir Robert we are here on official police business."

"Of course, sir. If you'd like to take a seat in the drawing room."

Albert and I didn't have long to wait before both Robert and Harriet entered.

"Commissioner, this is most unexpected. What can I do for you? Hobbes said it was a police matter. I thought the case had all but been solved? And, Miss Bridges, while it's always a pleasure to see you, in what capacity are you here? Not as a policeman obviously."

"As a matter of fact, Sir Robert, Miss Bridges is indeed here in an official capacity. She is now in the employ of Scotland Yard as a consultant detective," Albert said.

"My dear Isobella, I'm astonished," said Harriet, coming over to greet me. "Although I really shouldn't be, should I? I always said you were sharp enough to cut yourself."

"Good god," muttered Robert. "Women detectives, whatever next?"

"Sir Robert, we would like to talk to you privately in a moment, just a few points needing clarification. But first, purely for elimination purposes, Miss Bridges will need to take both your and Miss Dinworthy's fingerprints."

As I readied my cards and ink, Robert spoke harshly to Albert.

"No, I'm afraid this won't do at all, Commissioner. I refuse to be treated as a suspect, especially in my own home."

"I'm afraid you are a suspect, Sir Robert," Albert said succinctly. "And if you'd prefer, we can always do this at Scotland Yard, although I admit the surroundings will be far less comfortable."

"How dare you come in here and treat Harriet and me like this? Neither of us had anything to do with Patty-Mae's murder. It's preposterous and I shan't have anything to do with it."

"It's not a request, Sir Robert," said Albert, and for the second time I saw his eyes turn to hard cold flint.

Harriet gently laid a hand on Robert's arm. "It will be perfectly all right, Robert, you'll see. And I'm afraid we really have no say in the matter. It's to eliminate us, my dear, not to accuse us. Look, I'll go first. Isobella, are you ready?"

I nodded and watched as Robert resigned himself. Harriet certainly had a calming effect on him and I thought again what a shame it had been the two hadn't married.

Once Harriet had witnessed her fingerprint cards with signature and date, I called for Robert.

He grudgingly gave me his left hand and I began the inking process. "Just how am I supposed to remove this infernal stuff?" he muttered. Even though Harriet had made him see sense, he was still incredibly annoyed. He was an old man, set in his ways and chary in his acceptance of change, especially when it came to women in the workplace. I mistakenly tried to appease him.

"It's rather like clerical work, Sir Robert. Just think of me as a secretary of sorts."

"Please don't patronise me, Miss Bridges."

I straightened and looked him squarely in the eye. "Then I would appreciate it if you would award me the same respect, Sir Robert."

He met my gaze for a moment, then gave a curt nod and looked away. Hardly a resounding success, but I'd take what little victory I could.

With the fingerprint cards completed and safely stored in my case, Harriet left the room and Albert and I continued our questioning of Robert. Albert didn't hold back as I'd expected him to, but launched straight to the heart of the matter.

"Sir Robert, were you aware Patty-Mae Ludere was a fraud? That the woman to whom you were engaged was a made up caricature by someone entirely different?"

I held my breath, waiting for vehement denials and protestations, but they never came. Instead Robert sat calmly and gave first Albert, then myself, a shrewd look. The silence seemed eternal and he was obviously not intending to speak. I surmised he was waiting to see exactly how much we knew before imparting his own knowledge.

"So how did you find out?" I asked. "Was it in the letters the postmaster gave you from America? I suppose a man of your wealth and position would need to make sure of your future wife's credentials. Did you hire a firm of detectives over there?"

Robert bristled visibly. "You've obviously done your homework, Miss Bridges," he said in a sour tone. "Yes, I did employ someone to do a little research. However, every lead resulted in a blind alley. It was as though she didn't exist."

"So you employed someone at this end to find out more," said Albert. "One Mr. Entwhistle."

"I've already told you about Entwhistle, Commissioner."

"So you did, Sir Robert, but I've been doing a little research of my own and I'm afraid your version doesn't quite match my findings. Mr. Entwhistle is a Private Investigator specialising in, among other things, spousal infidelities."

Once again the conversation I'd overheard began to make more sense.

"When he arrived here the night of the dinner party, I distinctly heard the word fraud. He meant Patty-Mae, didn't he?" I said.

Robert shot from his seat, his face filled with fury. "My god, you were spying on me? A guest in my own home and you were snooping and sneaking about? Just who do you think you are?"

"Please do calm down. It was purely an accident. I got lost on my way to the powder room. Hobbes found me eventually, but not before I'd unwittingly heard part of your conversation. It most certainly wasn't deliberate. Nor would I have thought twice about it. It was no concern of mine. However, the murder of Patty-Mae changes all that, Sir Robert, and casts a different light on your conversation with Mr. Entwhistle, given the new context. How did you feel when you found out that Patty-Mae Ludere was a fraud?"

"For heaven's sake, woman, have you lost your wits? How do you think I felt? I was shocked and upset. At first I thought there must have been some sort of mistake. How could my dear sweet Patty-Mae be anything other than she claimed? And why would she go to all that trouble? But then Entwhistle confirmed the findings. I had every intention of ending the engagement quietly and privately after you had all left. But by then it was too late."

He resumed his seat, slumping dejectedly as though all the fight had left him, but I knew it was an act.

"But that wasn't all Entwhistle found out, was it? The 'other matter' was his discovering she was seeing someone else. Patty-Mae had a long-term lover, Sir Robert, one that in all likelihood she wouldn't give up even after you were wed. Surely that must have made you angry?"

I held my breath, heart hammering wildly. Had I pushed him too far? Out of the corner of my eye I saw

Albert lean forward slightly ready to intervene in case Robert turned fierce.

"Good god, you never give up, do you?" he roared, standing and taking a step toward me.

Albert was silently hovering at his elbow in an instant.

"Yes, I found out she had a lover and yes, I was furious. She'd lied to me and schemed behind my back to marry me for my money so that she and her inamorato could live in luxury. I've already found several items missing, which I assume she's sold to feather their nest."

I realised he didn't know Patty-Mae was an addict and in all probability had stolen the items to purchase drugs.

"She'd made me look like a pathetic fool in front of my peers and a laughing stock in the village. Even my staff were giving me pitying looks. Oh yes, don't think I didn't see them. Her actions were unforgivable."

"So you killed her?" I ventured.

He leaned toward me, fists and teeth clenched, spittle collecting at the corner of his mouth and eyes consumed with rage.

"And what if I did?" he hissed.

Albert and I looked at each other. Was this a confession? Before we could ask, Harriet rushed through the door to Robert's side.

"No, don't listen to him. Robert didn't kill Patty-Mae. I did."

Robert looked at Harriet in shock. "No, Hettie." Turning back to us he said, "Don't listen to her. She's trying to protect me."

"Ahem." We all glanced at the door where Hobbes was standing.

"I'm afraid neither Sir Robert nor Miss Dinworthy could have killed Miss Ludere," he said.

"And why is that, Hobbes?" asked Albert.

"Because it was, in fact, I who carried out the murder."

CHAPTER TWENTY-THREE

Albert threw up his hands in despair.

"What on Earth do you people think this is, some sort of parlour game?"

Nobody said a word.

"You do all realise we will find the true culprit eventually? No matter who you think you are protecting, the truth will come out."

Still, they all remained stubbornly silent. What a ridiculously tangled web this was turning out to be. At that moment Phantom chose to make an appearance, weaving his way in a figure eight around the legs of Harriet, then Robert and finally Hobbes. Was this supposed to be some kind of message? If so, it was far too cryptic for me to understand.

"That's not in the least bit helpful, you know," I admonished him, then looked up to see everyone staring.

"I mean all this nonsense, everybody confessing. It's not helping matters," I concluded, abashed.

"Right, everybody take a seat. No one is allowed to leave this room until I say so," Albert said. "Ella, remain with them please. I have a phone call to make. Oh, and get Hobbes' fingerprints."

I did as he asked, then took in the scene. Robert and Harriet sat opposite each other near the fire, while Hobbes, uncomfortable at being made to sit, perched on a hard chair by the door. I looked at Harriet, but she refused to meet my eye. *Guilt?* Could my dear friend really have it in her to kill another person? I glanced at Robert staring furiously into the flickering flames. Did he really kill Patty-Mae? And Hobbes loyal to a fault, was he simply protecting his master and friend or were those the hands of a man capable of strangling a woman? I found I didn't know the answer to any of my questions and by the time Albert returned, I was feeling quite dizzy.

"Your attention, please. I have arranged for round the clock police presence. They will be here shortly. Each man is under strict instructions not to allow anyone to leave or enter the premises without my or Miss Bridges' permission. As of this moment, you are all under house arrest."

Robert looked up as though to argue, but Albert cut him off. "Just be thankful I'm not dragging you all back to the city cells for wasting police time."

Once Albert's men had arrived and been fully briefed, we took our leave and returned to the cottage. It was late and we were exhausted, but neither of us could contemplate sleep at that moment. So with a fire crackling in the hearth, I poured us both a nightcap.

"I have to admit in all my years dealing with the law, Ella, I have never come across a case where almost every suspect confesses to the crime. It's sheer lunacy."

"I can't understand what they all hope to achieve? We have Harriet protecting Robert, Robert protecting Harriet, and Hobbes protecting them both. Surely they realise it's only a matter of time before we find out who was really responsible?"

"Unfortunately, we are now reliant on one thing and one thing only. That Mortimer is successful in determining the owner of the print from the button. If he fails, and if our suspects continue with this folly, then I'll have no choice but to arrest and charge them all."

Bright and early the next morning, I was awoken by the ringing of the telephone. Grabbing my gown, I rushed down the stairs to answer it.

"Ella, it's Mortimer. Good news, I have the print from the button."

"That's marvellous. Albert and I will be there shortly. Thank you."

I replaced the receiver and called up the stairs. "Albert?"

"Here, Ella," he said, coming out of the dining room with a slice of toast in his hand. Mrs. Shaw must have already laid breakfast. "What is it?"

"That was Mortimer. He's managed to extract the print from the button. I said we'd be there shortly."

"Excellent. We'll leave within the hour."

An hour and a half later we were outside Mortimer's laboratory at Scotland Yard.

"Well, the time has finally arrived, Ella. Now we'll find out who our murderer is."

I nodded and took a deep breath as Albert opened the door.

"Ah, Commissioner, Ella. Right on time," Mortimer said. "Ella, I trust you've brought the fingerprint cards?"

I nodded and handed over my kit.

"Good, good. If you'll follow me."

We accompanied him through a door to the rear of the laboratory, where inside we found racks of shelving with small white cards in various slots, and a number of officers examining them through magnifying glasses. From a box marked 'Arundel Hall Murder: Evidence', he extracted two envelopes: one containing the button with its singular monogram, and the other a piece of white card with a fingerprint on it.

"We were very lucky to be able to lift this print. We found it on the reverse of the button and although it's only a partial of the whole, I believe it to be the mark of the perpetrator's right thumb."

I peered closely at the card and saw the familiar mass of ridges and whorls. Mortimer laid the card with the singular print at the top of the desk and placed the four cards of the suspects below. It would be impossible to discern a match with the naked eye, but Mortimer was already clutching a single magnifying lens in his right hand.

"It will take some time to identify the correct print. You're welcome to stay and wait, of course, but feel free to help yourselves to coffee or take a walk while I work."

I glanced at Albert. I didn't want to leave. My stomach was in knots and I was impatient for the results, but there seemed little sense in my loitering around and getting underfoot. Albert was of the same opinion. We could be of no practical help, so we adjourned to a small tea-room around the corner to await the runner Mortimer had promised to send as soon as he had news.

Several cups of tea, a toasted tea-cake and a small iced fancy later, a breathless boy, no older than fourteen, rushed to our table.

"Begging your pardon, sir, Miss. Doctor Smythe says he's ready for you now."

Albert thanked him and gave him tuppence.

"Run back and tell Doctor Smythe we're on our way, there's a good lad."

A few minutes later we were back at The Yard.

"So what do you have for us, Mortimer?" asked Albert.

"Here's your murderer," he replied, gesturing to the solitary card which remained with the print from the button.

"You're quite sure?"

"Absolutely certain. There's no doubt it's the same print."

I slowly walked toward the table, my heart beating frantically. Half of me wanted to know, the other half was afraid of what I would see.

Taking a deep breath, I glanced at the name and all the air whooshed out of my lungs.

"Oh, dear god," I whispered, groping behind me for the chair as my legs buckled. Albert put a comforting hand on my shoulder.

"Are you all right, Ella?"

"How could I have been so wrong about a friend?" I whispered.

"It happens to the best of us, my dear. But the first time is a terrible shock. I am truly sorry."

I nodded, the stirrings of anger beginning in my chest. There was no point becoming lachrymose. That would have to wait. Nor would second guessing myself help. We had a murderer to catch. I looked up.

"Albert, we need to finish this once and for all, and I have a plan."

We thanked Mortimer, took the evidence and retired to Albert's office for a meeting to fine tune the details. Albert made several phone calls to arrange for his men to tie up the loose ends and retrieve the additional information we would need. Finally, after three fraught hours in which I must have paced the equivalent of several miles, one of his men returned with a report confirming our suspicions, and I made a telephone call.

"Nathaniel, it's Ella. I'm calling to ask you a favour."

"I'll try, but I'm rather tied up with appointments at present. What did you need?"

"Could you find someone else to cover your appointments, do you think? We've found the murderer of Patty-Mae and we could do with a doctor at The Hall when we make the arrest. I rather think it's going to be a shock and we may need medical assistance."

There was a slight pause before he answered. "Yes, I think I can re-arrange a few things. I take it I'm no longer a suspect?"

"No, you're not a suspect, Nathaniel. Shall we say outside the gates in a couple of hours? I'd rather we all arrived together so as not to forewarn those inside?"

"Of course, I'll see you then."

"Thank you, Nathaniel," I said and replaced the receiver.

Albert rose and gathered the reports and evidence we'd need, and we stopped to release Edgar Rutherford on our way out. He'd also accompany us to The Hall for what I hoped would be the last time.

CHAPTER TWENTY-FOUR

Nathaniel was already parked at the gates of Arundel Hall when the three of us arrived, and followed in his own car as we made our way up the drive to the front door.

Albert told Hobbes we would be in the library and to ask Sir Robert and Harriet to join us.

Once we were all present, the doors to the library closed and guarded outside by two constables, Albert urged everyone to take a seat, Hobbes included, and standing with his back to the fire, addressed his audience.

"There has been in my experience several cases where there was more than one viable suspect for a crime, but never have I come across a group of people so intent on muddying the waters that half of them confessed to murder. A more ludicrous state of affairs, I can't imagine.

I warned you then I would find the perpetrator and I have gathered you all here this evening to inform you I have been successful. I now know who murdered Miss Patty-Mae Ludere."

As Albert spoke, I glanced at the faces of those present. Edgar, seated alone by the window, over which the heavy red velvet curtains were drawn, looked pale and exhausted. The time spent in the city cells had knocked every ounce of arrogance from his demeanour. No longer was he filled with blustering bravado; now he appeared small and tired, and very young. We'd given him no indication in the car as to the reason he'd been released and brought to The Hall, and his eyes flicked toward Albert with interest at the pronouncement the murderer had been identified.

The eyes of both Harriet and Robert had never left Albert from the moment he'd begun to speak. They were sat together on the sofa to his right, hands clasped and eyes wary. Robert's face indicated bubbling anger just below the surface and I felt he could erupt at any moment. Harriet, on the other hand, was wound as tight as a bowstring and looked as though she might bolt at the earliest opportunity.

In complete contrast, Nathaniel sat opposite them, the epitome of relaxation, long legs stretched out in front of him and one arm strewn across the back of the sofa. He rewarded my glance with a wink and a small smile.

As was his custom as a servant, Hobbes had chosen to remain seated by the door. Stoical as ever, the only indication of his discomfort was the tightening of his jaw and the narrowing of his eyes at the mention of the murderer.

"Sir Robert and Miss Ludere," Albert continued, "met at a ball held at The Dorchester several months ago. However, during the course of this inquiry, it has come to light this was no chance meeting. It was in fact instigated deliberately by Miss Ludere herself and Mr. Rutherford."

All eyes swung to Edgar as he visibly shrank in his chair, refusing to meet anyone's gaze. Robert's eyes were murderous as he glared at Edgar.

"Why, you despicable..." he began, but was stayed by Harriet's hand.

"A man in Sir Robert's position would naturally need to know more about his future wife, so prior to the engagement he enlisted the help of a detective agency in America. A short time later he received word that no trace of her could be found. Miss Patty-Mae Ludere did not in fact exist."

Edgar put his head in his hands and groaned softly, realising no doubt that the scheme he and Martha had painstakingly put together would never have worked. This was most definitely news to Nathaniel, Harriet, and Hobbes, however, as I noticed their surprise at the revelation.

Albert continued, "Thus, perturbed at the news, Sir Robert went on to hire the services of a Private Investigator in London. He followed Miss Ludere on several occasions and subsequently discovered not only was she a fraud, but she was also in a long-term relationship with another man." Albert paused and looked at Sir Robert. "I assume your man Entwhistle, while describing her lover to you, was unable to give you his name?"

Robert nodded curtly. "It was a generic description and could have been any one of a dozen dandies. I know damn well who it was now though. It was you, Rutherford!" he bellowed, a shaky hand pointing in Edgar's direction.

"Indeed," said Albert. "But if there was no such person as Patty-Mae Ludere, then just who was she?"

All eyes, bar Edgar's, turned back to Albert.

"Her true name was Martha Brown and she was formerly a singer, dancer and hostess at a notoriously bawdy club in London."

Robert went white with shock. Harriet's sharp intake of breath was audible as she clutched her breast, and Nathaniel blurted out, "I don't believe it." Even the news had shocked Hobbes enough for him to momentarily lose his mannequin-like pose.

"But I'm afraid that's not all. Martha, or Patty-Mae as you knew her, was an opiate addict."

Robert rose suddenly and shakily made his way to the drinks tray, where he poured himself a stiff whiskey, downed it in one gulp, and then immediately poured another.

"I can tell from your reaction you were unaware of these additional facts, Sir Robert. Regardless, you had both the motive and the opportunity to commit the murder. You had already discovered Miss Ludere was not the American heiress and well-known actress she claimed to be. Moreover, you had noticed several small and expensive items had gone missing since her arrival. The final straw came on the evening of the dinner when your investigator came to give his report, and informed you that not only was she a fraud, but she was involved with another. In your own words," and here Albert took out his black notebook, "'She'd made me look like a pathetic fool in front of my peers and a laughing stock in the village. Even my staff were giving me pitying looks. Her actions were unforgivable.' A huge loss of face, I agree, Sir Robert, but enough to commit murder? You had plenty of time on the night of the dinner, after Entwhistle had left, to enter the garden, find Miss Ludere and strangle her, then appear back in the library. Then later on, of course, you confessed.

"But let us move on for a moment because you were not the only one to admit to the murder. Nor, in fact, were you the only one to have the motive and opportunity to commit the crime."

Here Albert glanced at me to continue, but I shook my head. Perhaps it was cowardly of me, but I didn't want to be the one to air Harriet's secrets in public. She'd been my friend. So Albert continued.

"Miss Dinworthy, you have known Sir Robert since you were children and recently admitted you've been in love with him for most of your life. In fact, you said yourself your families expected you to marry. It must have been difficult for you when he returned from the war with a wife on his arm? Surely, however, when she passed away your chance had finally come? But no, once again you were cast aside when it was announced Sir Robert had become betrothed to Miss Ludere. But of course that's not the whole story, is it? On the night of the dinner, Miss Ludere approached you in the powder room and told you in no uncertain terms to leave Sir Robert alone. Even she could see how obvious your true feelings were. Naturally, when cornered you came out fighting, you said, and gave her a piece of your mind, a few home-truths as it were. But I posit you could have taken it one step further and killed her in a jealous rage. Returning to the library, you found Miss Bridges and Doctor Brookes already there, but Miss Bridges left shortly afterward, leaving you alone with the doctor. At your request he went to his car to retrieve a mild sedative for your nerves, which gave you plenty of time to seek out Miss Ludere in the garden, strangle her and return with no one the wiser. Let's not forget Miss Ludere had consumed a lot of alcohol that evening and was already unsteady. It would have been quite easy for you to subdue her. And then, as with Sir Robert, you also confessed to the crime."

Albert once again glanced at me, and this time I was happy to take up the reins.

"Not long before the dinner here, Doctor Brookes visited me in a professional capacity. During that visit, I found a note in his bag saying 'PM police'. Initially, I thought it indicated an evening appointment he had, but upon questioning, Doctor Brookes informed us the PM did in fact pertain to Patty-Mae. As you've already been informed, she was addicted to opiates, and as her supplier was no longer available to her, she sought out Doctor Brookes in the hope he would be able to give her the drug she craved. Doctor Brookes categorically refused, but told us he intended to seek out the police once he'd done a little investigation of his own. But is that simply the end of the matter or was there something more sinister happening? Perhaps Patty-Mae pestered him so much he could no longer stand it. Or could she have threatened him in some way? Or perhaps her propositions were more amorous in nature? Whatever the reasons, Doctor Brookes also had the opportunity to rid himself of the victim when he left to retrieve the sedative for Harriet. His car was parked at the back and it would only have been a matter of minutes for him to reach Patty-Mae at the side of the house, kill her and return to the library. But while the opportunity was there, is this really a strong enough motive to take a life? And wouldn't it also go against everything a doctor is supposed to stand for?"

I turned to Hobbes.

"Hobbes, you've been with Sir Robert for a long time now. Originally as his batman, you then came here to act as his butler and valet. I also surmise you were a much-needed friend and companion, particularly during the years after the death of his first wife. Your loyalty to him is without question, which is why, I believe, you also confessed to the murder. Rather than allow Robert to be convicted for a crime to which he'd confessed, you would quite happily take his place as a final act of friendship, not least because Robert saved your life during the war. But did you in fact kill Miss Ludere? You certainly had the opportunity, knowing the house and its short-cuts as well as you do, and of course a good servant goes about his business silently and unobtrusively, hardly noticed by those in the house. But what could be your motive? Well, of course, that's simple. Patty-Mae had used Robert in the most horrible of ways and I suspect you also overheard the report from Entwhistle, but being privy to Robert's life in a way I was not, you knew immediately whom they were talking about. Deciding to save Robert from the future anguish of having such a wife, you took it upon yourself to get rid of her. So you had both the motive and the opportunity. But are you really the one we are looking for, or is it someone else?"

I looked back to Albert who nodded and once again took up the narrative.

"Mr. Rutherford has already spent time in the city cells for this crime. He admitted to arguing with and striking Miss Ludere, and the missing button from his shirt was found in her dead hand. Compelling evidence, as I'm sure you'll agree. But from the start, he has maintained his innocence and while he may be guilty of many other crimes, he is in fact wholly innocent of this one. Edgar Rutherford did not murder the woman known as Patty-Mae Ludere. But one of you sitting before me here tonight, did."

CHAPTER TWENTY-FIVE

All eyes turned toward Albert, the change in the atmosphere palpable, charged with a crackling of expectation, tinged with fear. It lifted the hairs on the back of my neck and despite the heat from the fire, I shivered. We all knew the time had finally come to unveil the murderer.

"Doctor Brookes, your explanation of the note Miss Bridges saw was that you were going to speak to the police about Patty-Mae, correct?"

Nathaniel frowned. "Yes."

"But it didn't mean that at all, did it?" I asked.

Nathaniel turned to face me.

"What do you mean, Ella?"

"I mean you lied. What the note actually meant was completely the opposite. Patty-Mae was going to the police about you! She'd stumbled upon your secret, Nathaniel, and I suspect she tried to blackmail you into supplying her drugs in return for her silence."

"What? Of course not, that's ridiculous. What on Earth could she blackmail me about? I'm a simple village doctor." He stood up and took a step toward me.

I took an involuntary step back.

"No, you're not. You failed to qualify and fraudulently took over your father's practice. Who would know, considering you shared the same name? And why would people not believe you? You are the son of an honest and respected man and expected to follow in his footsteps. But that's not all. You've been selling drugs in the city. Patty-Mae found out, as Martha Brown it was her real world, after all. You killed her, Nathaniel. You are the murderer we have been looking for."

I heard the gasps of shock behind me, but my eyes never left Nathaniel's.

He held out his hands placatingly, "Ella, this is nonsense. You have no proof…"

Albert interrupted before he could finish.

"That's where you're wrong, Doctor Brookes. Do you really think we would make these accusations without proof?" Albert lifted from his case the report his officers had given him earlier.

"We have here sworn statements from a number of people to whom you sold drugs. Each one of them has formally identified you from a photograph."

"And you'd take the word of prostitutes and drug addicts over mine, a well-respected doctor? They are lying," Nathaniel scoffed.

"We also have statements from the head of your college and several tutors stating you failed the final examinations. You are not in fact a registered doctor, you are a cheat."

"There were extenuating circumstances, which are none of your business. I fully intend to re-sit my examinations in due course. It's purely a formality. However, none of this means I killed Miss Ludere."

"No, it doesn't," I said. "But it was your motive for doing so."

"But, Ella, surely you don't believe all this. I thought we had something between us. You said yourself on the telephone I was no longer a suspect."

"But don't you understand, Nathaniel? You are no longer a suspect because you are the murderer, and here is the proof." I held up the two fingerprint cards.

"These are your fingerprints, the ones I took, remember? And this ..." I held up the second card, "is the print from the back of the shirt button taken from Patty-Mae's hand. They are a perfect match, Nathaniel, and only her murderer could have placed that button after her death."

I should have seen the intention in his eyes then, but I missed it. Suddenly, he lunged forward, knocking me to the floor and sprinting for the door. Wrenching it open, he came face to face with the two constables, but before they could act, Edgar had sprung from his chair, tackled him to the floor and punched him in the face.

"That's for Martha, you murdering bas ... "

"Enough!" bellowed Albert. "Constables, place Doctor Brookes under arrest and take him back to The Yard."

Albert grabbed Edgar by his collar and hauled him to his feet.

"Take a seat, Edgar. It's over."

Hobbes had come to my assistance the moment I was knocked to the ground and helped me stand on shaking legs. I could already feel the beginnings of a bruise on my cheek.

Harriet and Robert clung to each other, struck dumb by the revelations and the subsequent violence. It was difficult to see who was holding up whom.

After Nathaniel had been unceremoniously thrust into the rear of the police vehicle and was on his way back to Scotland Yard, the rest of us gathered together in the library once more.

"Nathaniel Brookes. I can't believe it," said Harriet. "It will be the death of his poor father. He's already in precarious health, so I understand."

"So Brookes was supplying Patty-Mae drugs?" asked Robert.

I shook my head. "No, I don't think he was. I'm sure that part of his story was true. It was too close to home to risk it. He wouldn't want to soil his own patch, as it were. He would have been caught. No, he preferred the anonymity of the city; I hate to think how long it's been going on. Certainly over a year, if the statements are anything to go by."

"He must have been planning to kill her that night," said Edgar.

"I don't believe so, Edgar," said Albert. "This was not a premeditated murder. He saw an opportunity that night and took it. But if it hadn't been that night then I'm sure it would have been another. Martha's threat was very real and he needed to stop her once and for all. Overhearing the two of you arguing was convenient, and finding your button to throw us off the scent was a stroke of good fortune as far as he was concerned."

"Oh, god, it's all my fault. If we hadn't argued … "

"If you hadn't dreamed up this diabolical scheme in the first place, none of it would have happened," snapped Robert.

"Edgar," I said, "if you hadn't argued and lost your button, then we wouldn't have caught him at all. All the other evidence was circumstantial. The only thing we caught him on was the fingerprint. He would have killed her eventually and while it's no solace to you, at least this way he will be tried and punished for the crime."

Edgar didn't speak, but nodded dejectedly. I doubted he would ever get over his loss, but I hoped he would find a better way of living his life in the future.

"I think it's time we left, Ella," Albert said, rising. "I'll drop you at your cottage as I intend to go straight back to London."

I nodded and also rose to gather my belongings.

"Edgar, will you be staying on at Linhay or at your London Apartment? I'll drop you either way."

"I'll come to London. Thanks."

At the door, Robert held out his hand to Albert. "Thank you, Commissioner."

"Goodbye, Sir Robert," he said, shaking the proffered hand. "Miss Dinworthy."

Harriet smiled and said goodbye, then turned to me."Isobella, perhaps we could have tea together soon?" she asked in a tentative tone.

I smiled. "I'd like that, Harriet, thank you."

"Splendid. I'll telephone you."

Albert dropped me at my cottage and within moments of my head hitting the pillow, I was fast asleep.

CHAPTER TWENTY-SIX

arriet's call to tea came several days later and as Hobbes drove closer to The Hall, I saw there were several moving vehicles being packed with boxes.

"Good heavens, Harriet, is Robert moving?" I asked as she came to greet me.

"Actually, Isobella, we both are."

It was then I noticed how well she looked. Happy and glowing and …

"Harriet, you got married?" I asked, spying the rings.

She nodded. "Yes, we did, yesterday. Just a small registry office affair. It was all we wanted."

"Oh, that's wonderful news, Harriet, congratulations. I really am so very happy for you."

"Thank you, my dear. Come inside and I'll tell you all about it over tea."

Harriet took us to a small, bright and cheerful sitting room at the back of the house with a splendid view of the gardens. The sun was dazzling and I could just make out the glint of the lake in the distance along with the small figure of Robert walking his dogs. After Harriet had told me about the wedding, I asked her where they were moving to.

"Everywhere. We've decided to travel the world, starting in Europe and then moving where the fates decide. Certainly to Africa, we both have a desire to visit Kenya and Egypt. The world is a huge place, Isobella, and we're not getting any younger."

"So what about The Hall? Is it to be sold?"

"It is, although it will be some time before it's ready to be put on the market. Hobbes has agreed to stay and oversee the sale of the contents, particularly the rare wines and the other items in the hidden cellars. They're all worth rather a lot of money as it turns out. He'll also look after the dogs and whatnot, then when he's ready, he's free to join us if he wishes, wherever that may be. In all honesty, I don't feel I would ever be comfortable living here and Robert feels the same."

"Because of Patty-Mae?" I asked.

"Partly yes, but the house has an ominous history, as you well know, and now we've finally found each other, I don't want to put our marriage at risk in any way."

"You mean the curse? I didn't think you really believed in it."

"Well, as I said before, as an historian I work with facts and figures, but considering all that happened previously and of course the most recent tragedy, I find I can't simply dismiss it."

"So when are you leaving? And what about your home?"

"Actually, this is goodbye, Isobella, we are heading up to London this evening and we leave England the day after tomorrow. As for my home, it's already occupied. I needed someone to live there long term and look after it in my absence, so I've given it to Mrs. Parsons and her husband. Tom will live there with them of course. They rented their little fisherman's cottage and it was just too dark and damp for them all, but particularly for Mr. Parsons whose health is deteriorating rapidly. At least this way he can live out the remainder of his days in comfort. I've also bequeathed both it and an annual income to them in my will, so if anything happens to me, they will still be looked after and have a roof over their heads."

I found I was inordinately pleased Harriet had been so generous to the Parsons. They were a good family and deserved some good fortune.

"And what about Mrs. Butterworth? I daresay she'll be at a bit of a loose end with only herself and Hobbes to cook for," I said.

"Oh, she intends to retire when Hobbes leaves. Robert has given her enough money to purchase a small cottage on Linhay. She's been a faithful member of staff, it's the least he could do. To be honest I think she found catering for the dinner party by herself a bit too much."

"Whatever do you mean, Harriet? I sent Mrs. Shaw up to assist. Was she of no help at all?"

"Oh, dear, forgive me for speaking out of turn, Isobella. It completely slipped my mind Mrs. Shaw is your housekeeper."

"Harriet, you must tell me what happened."

Harriet sighed deeply. "Well, between you and me, Mrs. Butterworth informed me Mrs. Shaw was completely ignorant of catering such a specialised menu. Her exact words were, 'if she used to cater for posh dinner parties in London, then I'll eat my apron so I will'. I am sorry, Isobella."

I forced a smile, but my mind was a whirl. "Don't worry, Harriet. I'm sure there's a simple explanation. I'll talk to her when I get back."

Harriet patted my hand and we continued to talk for a while about how Robert had given Edgar enough money to organise the funeral of Martha Brown and other, more inconsequential things until it was my time to depart.

As Hobbes was bringing the motorcar round to the front, Harriet hugged me and gave me a powdery kiss on both cheeks.

"Goodbye, Isobella, it really has been such a pleasure to know you. I'll write and send you postcards from our travels and do keep up your detective work. You really are very good at it."

I assured her I would, then with final farewells I left to go home.

When I arrived, with the intention of immediately speaking to Mrs. Shaw regarding Harriet's revelation, I found Albert sitting in the drawing room with a snifter of whiskey.

"Albert, how lovely to see you. I wasn't expecting a visit today or I would have made sure I was at home."

Albert waved a dismissive hand. "Don't worry, Ella, I've not been here long. I had an appointment with Doctor Brookes Senior to bring him up to date, so thought I'd take the opportunity to see you while I was here."

At that moment the telephone rang.

"Sorry, Albert, do excuse me a moment."

I went to the hall and picked up the receiver just as Mrs. Shaw came to answer it.

"Hello?"

"Ella? Is that you? Ella, can you hear me?"

I was instantly weak and my legs began to give way as though my bones had liquefied and could no longer support me. A cold rush of sweat ran up my back and across my shoulders, and I clutched the edge of the table as my peripheral vision began to turn black.

In the far off distance I heard a voice call out, "Commissioner, come quick!"

My last thought before my world went dark was, 'impossible'. For the voice on the other end of the phone was unmistakably John's, my husband who had been dead for the last two years.

J. New is the author of The Yellow Cottage Vintage Mysteries, traditional English whodunits with a twist, set in the 1930's. Known for their clever humour as well as the interesting slant on the traditional whodunit, they have all achieved Bestseller status on Amazon.

J. New also writes the Finch and Fischer contemporary cozy crime series and (coming in 2021) the Will Sharpe Mysteries set in her hometown during the 1960's. Her books have sold over one hundred-thousand copies worldwide.

Jacquie was born in West Yorkshire, England. She studied art and design and after qualifying began work as an interior designer, moving onto fine art restoration and animal portraiture before making the decision to pursue her lifelong ambition to write. She now writes full time and lives with her partner of twenty-one years, two dogs and five cats, all of whom she rescued.

If you enjoyed *The Curse of Arundel Hall* in the *The Yellow Cottage Vintage Mysteries*, please consider leaving a review on Amazon.

If you would like to be kept up to date with new releases from J. New, you can sign up to her *Reader's Group* on her website www.jnewwrites.com You will also receive a link to download the free e-book, *The Yellow Cottage Mystery*, the short-story prequel to the series.

Made in the USA
Columbia, SC
07 June 2024

36760365R00155